Always Hiding

Always Hiding

A Novel

Sophia G. Romero

William Morrow and Company, Inc.

New York

It is the policy of Willilam Morrow and Company, Inc., and its imprints and affiliates, recognizing the importance of preserving what has been written, to print the books we publish on acid-free paper, and we exert our best efforts to that end.

Library of Congress Cataloging-in-Publication Data

Romero, Sophia G.
    Always hiding : a novel / by Sophia G. Romero.
      p. cm.
    ISBN 0-688-15632-0
    I. Title.
  PS3568.05647A79   1998
  813'.54—dc21   97-16192
                                                CIP

Printed in the United States of America

First Edition

1 2 3 4 5 6 7 8 9 10

BOOK DESIGN BY M. KRISTEN BEARSE
www.williammorrow.com

For Dan,
ang tangi kong Mahal

Acknowledgments

I AM PROFOUNDLY INDEBTED to the following institutions and individuals who kept vigil with me throughout this creative endeavor. Without their faith, friendship, and support, I doubt this novel would have ever been completed.

The Writers Room, New York City, New York

The Southold Public Library, Southold, New York

Judy Rossner and Valerie Sayers, who treated me as a peer long before I became theirs

Steven Borow, Peter Franck, Meg Cameron, Laurel Gross, Fran Hawthorne, and Tom Shachtman, who illuminated steps along the way

My agent, Wendy Weil, who believed

and my editor, Anne Freedgood, who saw and understood

"Know your roots and remember."

—F. SIONIL JOSE

Always Hiding

Prologue

L ast night, I really saw my mother's face for the first time. I had been so used to seeing it with makeup, and the starkness of its absence startled me. Her skin was pale and dry. The fine mesh of her complexion was an overlapping filigree of pain, sorrow, and sacrifice; each vein had its own story to tell. She had no eyebrows. Years of plucking them, shaping them into a finely arched bow, punishing an errant strand, had finally destroyed the entire population of tender follicles from which they grew. Without makeup, my mother's face was an empty canvas.

The longer I looked at her, the more I realized that I was watching her gradual decay. Without legal documentation, she was living the immigrant's nightmare: always hiding, always lying. She should never have left Manila. She must come back. I must do what I should have done a long time ago, what I have always done. I will bring her home.

—New York

1

My birth should have been an auspicious occasion for my parents because I was their first child. But I was born a girl, and in the Philippines, that made all the difference. I was cursed. Like all other daughters before me and all other daughters after me, I was cursed to suffer for my father's sins, whatever they were, for the rest of my life. Every single day of it.

I was born in Manila in 1969. My parents, Diosdado and Lourdes, named me Maria Violeta Rosario Dacanay after the Virgin Mary, my mother's favorite color, and the rosary. My mother wanted to call me Starshine for short, after the popular song "Good Morning, Starshine," which was the last song she heard just before they put her to sleep during labor. My father thought it was a ridiculous idea. "You might as well call her Full Moon since she was born during one," he supposedly ranted. They settled on Viola, although I don't think that being named after an instrument was any improvement. But I suppose that, of the many things they argued about later on, what to call me for short was the least of their problems.

We were not a wealthy family. At least, not in the beginning.

My parents ran a small bookstore that sold used books. My mother had inherited the business from her father, who used to sell them out of his *bodega,* a storage space in the house where they lived. Like me, my mother was an only child; she had lost her own mother at an early age and her father never remarried. She missed her mother; her father was too lost in his own grief and bitterness to look after her. "He never let me forget the injustice of it all: that I had lived and she had died," she told me.

My grandfather, an unlettered man, had discovered the musty old boxes of books while he was looking for a dead rat. At first he was going to throw them away, but he changed his mind when he saw that they were about foreign people and places. Some were even early editions of *National Geographic* magazine. He decided to sell them as valuable and irreplaceable antiques, supposedly saying, "What the people see doesn't matter. What matters is what they choose to believe."

During her sophomore year in college, my mother began working in the *bodega* during her free time. She dusted the books, organized them alphabetically, and dusted them again. Shortly after she graduated with a degree in education, and before she could even think of working anywhere else, her father put her to work full time as the cashier because, he said, he couldn't trust anyone else.

"I had no choice really," my mother always said, smiling as she told me the story. "He said that the bookstore belonged to our family, so I might as well learn as much as I could about it. He believed that working for others was a waste of time." Behind her smile I always felt a lingering sense of wistfulness for what she might have become.

One day she was surprised to find a stranger working in the store, a young man studying to be a lawyer. My grandfather had hired him to take over my mother's duties when she went from dusting to cashiering. That was how my parents met. *My mother married a servant.*

My grandfather died before I was born. My mother never explained the cause of his death to me, but through family gossip here and there I found out that he choked to death on a bite of cassava pie. When I asked my mother to confirm this, she said, "That's what happens when hatred has no place else to go." *What kind of answer was that?*

On my grandfather's death, my father, with the help of my mother, took over the business, moved from the *bodega,* and opened a store on San Lazaro Street in the Sampaloc district of Manila, where there were several universities. The bookstore was on the ground floor of a two-story house. We lived on the top floor. My father called the bookstore Libreria de San Lazaro because he said that the Spanish name would make it sound classy.

But it was not classy enough for him. He wanted to hit the big time, and he wanted to do it at once. "He was always insecure about not becoming a lawyer. About how he was basically a houseboy," was my mother's way of explaining his ambition and impatience. This was typical of her explanations for the way he grabbed her role as her father's rightful heir and made that right his own. But what could she do? She was now a wife and mother.

In 1972, shortly after President Ferdinand Marcos declared martial law, my father got himself a wealthy Chinese business partner, Mr. Tee Pak Long, who was supposed to be well connected with Marcos, though what that connection was exactly no one, including my father, knew. I remember my mother asking my father if Mr. Long could be trusted because it was well known that the Chinese dealt only with their own kind. He gave her a sharp look and told her not to interfere with his business decisions. With Long's money, my father opened a bigger bookstore, this time selling new books. He called it Galaxy Books because he said it sounded stateside. But to hear my mother talk, the name could very well have been a reference to the size and reach of my father's ego.

I knew even then that their marriage had all the symptoms of a bad ending. It was only a matter of time before they knew it themselves.

2

The earliest memory I have of my mother is the day I was sitting on her lap, my legs straddling her thighs, my head lying flat on her chest. I was nursing on her left breast. As my lips moved to and fro, I became aware that her milk had suddenly lost its sweetness. I lifted my head, opened my lips, and released her bosom.

"What's the matter, Viola?" my mother asked as she tried to press the back of my head closer to her chest. I pulled farther away.

"No more," I said.

"What do you mean, 'No moh'?" she asked, in a voice at once amused, patient, and, I thought, slightly dismayed. "Are you sure?"

I nodded quickly, turning my mouth away. She buttoned up her blouse, turned to my father, who was smoking nearby, and smiled. I never went back to her breast after that; I couldn't bear to be around milk.

I was two years old.

People laughed when I told them this story. At a family reunion where it was common practice to subject the youngest child to some form of torture, a drunken uncle offered me five pesos for a childhood memory. I went to the middle of the room unafraid, eager to tell my story, to get my five pesos. All I got was laughter. Harsh, mean laughter.

"How can anyone's memory go that far back?" everyone, including my parents, asked in disbelief. "You're just making it up, Viola," someone said. "It didn't happen," declared another. I never got the five pesos. But I did remember. I was five years old.

The exact circumstances of my birth were a blur in my mother's mind. Each time I asked her how I came to be her child, or how I was born, she always said in a vague, dreamy voice, "I don't remember," or "I don't know." Or she would weave a story as elaborate as her mood was that day.

"Oh, the bread man delivered you instead of the *pan de sal,*" she would declare enthusiastically, referring to the freshly baked buns daily delivered to our doorstep before sunrise. When that bored me, she would say, "We cracked an egg, and there you were, all curled up inside, sucking your thumb." When she told me these stories, she and I were always sitting together on the *perresoza,* the reclining chair she inherited from her mother, I on her lap, twirling my finger around her hair, my toes running up and down her thighs, giggling.

I liked her stories better than fairy tales. It didn't matter if she told me the same story again and again, or whether it was true or not. I always believed her. Mothers didn't lie. Once, when she snapped "I was asleep" during an account of my birth, I was shocked. Did she mean that I came out during her *siesta,* or that I slipped out in the middle of the night? For days afterward I couldn't close my eyes. I was afraid that a baby would crawl out of me when I wasn't looking.

"What's wrong with Viola?" my father asked my mother one night after dinner, looking over at me. I pretended not to hear them.

"What do you mean?"

"She's been walking around with a frown on her face. She won't even talk to me."

"Oh," my mother said, smiling, "she's been sulking ever since I told her that I was asleep when she was born."

"Because of *that*? Why didn't you tell her that when we went to the baby bank to ask for a girl with skin as brown and sweet as coconut jam, eyes the size of a full moon, hair as lush as the rice harvest in June, and a nose as delicate as a *gumamela* bud, they handed her to us all wrapped up and ribboned? Why didn't you tell her that?" He winked at me out of the corner of his eye, trying to salvage the impression that my mother had destroyed.

All she did was shrug her shoulders. My father shook his head in mock regret, walked over to where I was sitting, and put me on his lap. "Viola," he said, "let *me* tell you the real story of how you came to be our daughter."

But my father was not a storyteller; he obscured the truth. Early in my life I learned not to trust my father completely.

"Go away!"

"Viola!" my mother said sharply.

"Is that the way to talk to your father?" he asked.

I refused to answer.

Shocked and angry, he dropped me on the floor and swung his arm high above him, like a flyswatter ready for the kill.

"Dado, don't!" my mother screamed as I quickly got to my feet and ran to the door.

From behind me I heard my father say, "Where did she learn

to speak like that? She's been spending too much time with the maids."

"Well, if you were around more often instead of—"

I didn't wait for my mother to finish her sentence. At five years old, it hurt me to learn that my parents couldn't agree on how I was born.

3

I was seven when I realized that I was an only child. I had always been content to be the center of my parents' universe, the object of their and everyone else's affection, and the sole claimant to the territory right there between them in their bed.

It was not an unpleasant way to live; I considered brothers and sisters unwanted competition. I was never short of classmates and neighborhood playmates, and that was what maids were for. This changed when I discovered that I couldn't blame anyone else for the things I did, or sweet-talk my way out of trouble. I couldn't always rely on friends, who sometimes preferred the company of others. The maids were constantly eloping with every gardener who happened to glance their way, and their replacements were usually stupider than the last. Most of all, it got harder and harder to play all the roles of the Von Trapp children in *The Sound of Music.*

"For my next birthday I'd like to have a brother or sister instead of a party," I told my parents one night. Neither of them said anything, but underneath the covers the three of us shared, I felt my father's hairy leg grope for my mother's smooth calf on the opposite side of the bed.

"What do you mean?" he asked.

"I'm tired of being an only child. Do you think we could order a brother or sister from the same baby bank you got me?"

My mother laughed softly.

"Don't you like having us to yourself?" my father asked.

"It's not that. I just want to be with someone. You have each other. All my friends have brothers and sisters. I'm the only one without anybody."

"Hey, your dad and I don't have any brothers or sisters, do we, Dado?"

"That's different!" I protested. "You're not kids."

"But if we got you a brother or sister you'd have to share your things. You'd have to stop sleeping with us because we couldn't all fit in the bed," he said.

I sat up. "We can afford more toys and a new bed, can't we? I just want one other child, anyway. You don't have to get me more unless you really want to."

"Are you prepared to sleep in your own room?" my mother asked.

This baffled me. Sleeping with them had not been my idea in the first place. Every night, just before going to bed, my father would call to me from their bedroom, "It's lonely to be there all by yourself," or "Watch out for the *muumuu*. They'll bite off your toes!" When neither of these enticements worked, I would wake up the next morning to find myself lying between them just the same.

"You wouldn't mind, would you, Dad?"

"No, of course not. I'll miss you, but that's okay."

"I can always come back, right?"

"Sure!" they said at the same time.

"But, Viola," my mother whispered, "you must promise not to tell anyone about your brother or sister. Let's make it our secret, okay?"

"Why?"

"Well, for one thing, I don't know how quickly we can get a brother or sister for you. The baby bank may not have one available right away. And if other people find out, they might get jealous and steal one."

"There wouldn't be any left for us," my father added.

I had never kept a secret before. I suddenly felt like a grown-up. Without their realizing it, my parents had drawn me into their world. By embracing me as one of their own, they were telling me that I was no longer just their child. I was their equal.

"I promise."

The following days I walked around with a smile bigger than my face. A playmate would ask, "What's so funny, Viola?" and I would reply, "Oh nothing," and skip away, bubbling with confidence. I always remembered what my parents said and remained proudly tight-lipped.

As each day brought my birthday closer, I began to rehearse the role of sister. I strutted around in the manner of one born to be followed, whipping my imaginary sibling into shape with the wave of a barbecue stick. I dreamed of being older, bigger, smarter. Oh, the joy of being first!

I picked out a name for the other child in case he or she didn't come with one. If it was a boy, I would call him Iggy Boy, and if it was a girl, I would call her Cherry Pie. One of my friends had a sister named Apple Pie, and I wanted a pie of my own too. On my birthday, I woke up early. As my father was driving off for work, I chased after him and yelled, "Don't forget!"

It was a long Thursday, and a six-hour power interruption made the day seem endless. I hated these blackouts. What a time not to watch TV! Out on the streets I heard my playmates reciting a silly rhyme. In a moment of weakness, I almost broke into their circle, but I didn't want to end up all hot and sweaty. Grown-ups never lost their poise.

My mother invited me to join her on a short drive and enjoy the car air conditioner. To her surprise, I said no.

"Aren't you taking this a bit too seriously, Viola?" she asked.

How dare she say such a thing! Didn't she see this was an important day for me? I wanted to be in the house when my father returned home, to be the first one to see who he would bring back for me.

That evening, at the familiar rumble of his car, I dashed out to get a glimpse of the long-awaited sibling. But when he got out of the car, all he had with him was a funny grin and a huge black-and-white teddy bear wrapped in yellow cellophane.

"Where's my brother? Give me my sister!" I cried, jumping into the backseat. But there was nothing there except a pile of newspapers, a folding umbrella, and balls of used tissues. My father continued to stand there with the stuffed animal in his arms.

"That's not what I asked for!" I screamed and started to cry. My mother stepped forward to take me in her arms, but I backed away.

"The bank didn't have any brothers or sisters," she said. "But your daddy didn't want to disappoint you, so he came home with this. Wasn't that nice of him?"

"I didn't tell anyone about our secret! I swear I didn't! Did you?"

"No, of course we didn't, and I know you didn't either. But see how soft and cuddly this bear is. Why don't you sleep with it for tonight and see how you like it."

I hated the beast. Every time I moved, its plastic paws hit me in the face and its long nose poked me in the neck. In their bedroom, I could hear my parents arguing, my mother saying,

"You're such a failure!" I covered my ears and fell asleep on my bed. The bear lay somewhere on the floor.

Three days later, I heard my mother's excited voice calling out to me. *The baby is here,* I thought happily as I dashed down the stairs and into the garden where my parents were.

In the middle of our newly mowed lawn my father was playing with a tiny white-and-brown puppy. Next to my father was my mother, trying to balance herself in her high heels.

"Come over here, Viola, and meet Marble. Isn't she a cutie?" My father's fingers ran up and down her smooth, quivering belly. "Marble's a Boston bull terrier. See how friendly she is."

I remained where I was. I had asked for an Iggy Boy or a Cherry Pie, and all I got was a dog. My parents had lied. Right then and there, I decided I was better off not being part of my parents' world because there was nothing special about it after all. Grown-ups were just a bunch of people who were born first, made all sorts of rules, and destroyed them whenever they pleased. I vowed never to become a grown-up like them.

My mother was annoyed. "Oh, stop being so childish!"

"I am a child!"

"It's not every day that you get a dog."

When I still didn't move, she looked at my father, but he was playing with Marble. She took a deep breath and said, "She won't bite, you know."

"What if she does?" I asked as I finally allowed my mother to take my hand.

"Then we'll just have to give her away," said my father as the puppy rolled over and wagged her tail at me. I looked at her face, especially those large saucer eyes of hers smiling at me. Next thing I knew I was smiling back at her.

When Marble was less than a year old, my father ran over her as he was backing out of the driveway. My mother and I were standing by the front door, watching him leave. Suddenly, Marble appeared from one of the shrubs and scooted under the car. I heard a sharp yelp and tires shrieking to a stop. My mother pulled me quickly to her chest as her arms covered my eyes and ears, but Marble's voice wouldn't leave me. Through the gaps between my mother's fingers, I saw my father jump angrily out of the car, gesturing wildly as he dropped to the ground, looking for Marble. I tore away and followed the sound of Marble's whimpers growing fainter and fainter.

My father stood up, cradling her limp body, and gently transferred her into my arms. I bent down to nuzzle her neck the way I always used to when we slept together, but there was no wet tongue to lick my face. I carried her to the doghouse at the end of the garage and sat on the corner. My mother kept calling me, but I ignored her. I didn't even turn when my father came over and said, "Sorry."

I didn't blame my father for Marble's death; it was an accident. But shortly after she died, he began appearing in my room to find out how I was, to tell me a knock-knock joke he'd just learned, or he'd bring home a gift each time he returned from work. I noticed that he was coming home earlier than usual.

Then he began a question-and-answer routine, asking me whether I loved him or not. "Of course, Daddy," I would answer. He would smile and hug me close to him, but a few days later he would return and ask, "Who do you love more, Daddy or Mummy?" to which I would say, "I love you both." Once he surprised me with yet another version of the question: "Who would you rather have as your daddy, me or the president of the Philippines?"

"Of course you, Daddy. Why do you keep asking me all these questions? Do you think I don't love you enough?"

One look at his face, and I was sorry I had asked. "I don't want to lose you, Viola," was all he said.

• • •

The questions suddenly stopped. A week or two later, I happened to walk into my parents' bedroom and found my mother sitting on my father's lap. They looked as if they were having a good time.

"Come over here, Viola," my mother said, giggling, holding my father's face between her hands. "Now tell me, isn't this the face of George Hamilton?"

I looked at my father. His face was nowhere near George's.

"James Brown," I said.

My father just sat there quietly. He never asked me a question again.

4

I hated my nose. It was so flat that when I turned sideways, the only part of my profile one could see was an outline of my forehead sloping downward. "Like a steamroller had come along and run out of gas right between her eyes," relatives snickered.

"It's that native side of us," my father tried to explain to me after I came home in tears because someone in school had called me *pango*. Flat nose.

"Native?"

"It just means that we don't have any European or American blood."

"But you and Mom aren't *pango*. Look at me!"

"Viola, noses take time to grow. It doesn't happen overnight. Just look at yourself. Right now, you can barely touch my navel. In ten years, I'll bet you'll be taller than me.

"Isn't there anything I can do to make it grow faster?"

"You have what you have."

That was fine for him to say. He didn't have a flat nose. I wanted mine different, and I wanted it now.

Then one day I saw a playmate clip a clothespin on her nose.

I smuggled a couple into my room and clamped one onto the bridge of my nose. It pinched so hard that it broke in two. I rubbed my nose, wiped the tears, and tried again. The same thing happened. I tried for the third time and prayed for a miracle. This time it stayed on and didn't hurt as much.

I walked around with the clothespin, fighting the pain, ignoring the tears that ran down my face. I convinced myself that with each sting my nose was getting higher and higher, and by the end, I would come running out of my room, barge into my parents and show them my beautiful new nose.

None of it happened. After three days, my nose developed a severe infection, and I had to be rushed to the hospital because I had breathing difficulty. In the emergency room, a nurse inserted a needle to suck out the fluid that had blocked my nasal passages. The procedure lasted an hour because I couldn't sit still, and the needle kept falling out. I kept screaming, "Mummy! Daddy! Help me!" but they never came.

When it was over, I had a huge bandage on my nose. Instead of looking like Marie Osmond, I looked like Big Bird. I expected my parents to embrace me, shower me with congratulations for being such a brave girl, and treat me to an ice cream sundae. But they had something else in mind.

At home, my mother pinched me by my ear and dragged me down to kneel on the garage pavement. In the midst of her anger, she had grabbed a jar of rock salt, emptied its contents on the ground, and ordered me to kneel on top of the prickly layer and stretch out my arms, like Jesus Christ but without the nails and cross. As my mother circled around me, I was made to recite over and over, *"Ano ang parusa? Pagmamahal."* What is punishment? It is love.

I was on my knees for a long time, not allowed to cry or complain. The slightest whimper was met with a stern verbal rebuke from my father, who watched all this from his aluminum folding chair. I had to understand and accept the pain and suffering that came with being loved and being beautiful.

I wondered if it wasn't too late for George Hamilton to replace my father.

I was eight years old.

5

This is the house that Galaxy Books and Publishing built. With these words my father always welcomed first-time visitors to our house. This was the house we moved into six years after the business had grown beyond my father's expectations. It was not the house I was born in.

Our old house had a red brick exterior, an unpainted tin roof, and ornamental wrought-iron grillwork over the windows. Tied to one grille was a dried palm leaf that had been plaited into a fan of flowers, a remnant of Palm Sundays past. In the front yard, just outside the entrance to the bookstore, was a mango tree that my mother had planted shortly after I was born. It was a sapling from the tree that grew in her own mother's ancestral home, somewhere in a province outside of Manila.

As the mangoes ripened, their golden skins glistened in the branches, and passersby could not resist slinging rocks at them and noisily slurping on their prized, buttery pulp. On many occasions, my father attempted to thwart the trespassers, but to no avail: They were too quick-footed for him. He would swing a broom high about his head, his voice yelling loud and clear, "Get out! *Layas,* all of you!" In their rush to escape his advances, mango peelings and pits were dropped, leaving a trail of debris on our sidewalk.

I was sorry to leave that house. I remember how my mother pleaded with my father not to sell it. He said no, and I saw my mother bite her lower lip and avert her eyes. On our last day, as the movers were loading the last boxes into the moving truck, my mother took me with her as she caressed the southwest corner of the cement fence where she had buried her wedding *arras,* the silver coins of good fortune. Hand in hand, she and I walked as she said good-bye to each part of the house, each part of herself. We stopped at the mango tree and I watched my mother reach for the branch closest to her and break it off in one snap.

Yet to hear my father speak, one would think that even this new house was not good enough. We had barely settled down when he began talking about someday living "over there," *over there* in the fancy enclaves of the wealthy *mestizo* class where security guards made sure that outsiders stayed away.

My father was obsessed with the crowd that called each other Jake as they slapped each other's shoulders in greeting and uttered dirty words like *coño* and *puñeta* and made them sound like compliments. My father paid for membership at the exclusive Manila Polo Club and took up tennis so that he could say that so-and-so missed his backhand. He encouraged my mother to join various civic organizations, attend fashion shows, wear couturier clothing. Even I was dragged into his social expansion scheme. I was expected to get chummy with the children. Yet no matter how well known our bookstore was, or how hard my parents tried to socialize, neither of them could disguise the fact that we were upstarts. Our money did not bear the stench of old wealth. Anyone could see that our genealogy didn't go back to Europe.

Where we ended up wasn't so bad. It was an area so open

that by day passenger buses and *jeepneys* had no qualms about using the streets as quick detours in their city routes, sprinting from one destination to another, terrorizing residents and pedestrians with their maniacal driving, strangling them with gusts of carbon monoxide and soot.

Yet at night, when calm was restored to the music of chirping crickets and burping frogs, I heard the muffled footsteps of a worker coming home at the end of a long day. Or the *balut* vendor plying eight-week-old duck eggs, crying, *"Bahloot, bahloot,"* an invitation to a midnight meal.

Where we lived had no name. Our house was a sprawling bungalow, the biggest on the block. I was taught never to use the word *mansion* in public because my mother was very careful not to draw attention to our status. Besides, the size of our house spoke for itself. It was surrounded by twenty-foot cement walls rimmed with pieces of broken glass and barbed wire. Two bougainvillea plants flanked our gate, intertwining along the archway, their bright fuschia flowers forming a canopy of color.

Once inside, a narrow, winding path led to the house and its five bedrooms, each with its own bath and toilet, a den, a formal living and dining room, two kitchens, a small office for my father, and a three-car garage. I wanted a swimming pool, but my father insisted on a tennis court instead. He wanted the whole family to play tennis, although more often than not he only wanted us to applaud his moves.

In the far north corner of the garden there was a gazebo where I did my homework in the afternoons, or played house by myself or with the maids. I considered the gazebo a place where I could be alone. In this world, removed from everything else, my parents did not exist.

6

I got my period on the same day that I found out my father was a womanizer. I felt a part of me leave as the warm blood oozed out of my body. September was my favorite month because of the monsoon rains, the typhoons, floods, and blackouts. It was the only month when classes were suspended, so often it felt like a summer vacation.

For several days now, the newspapers, radio, and television had been discussing a storm that was making its way to Central Luzon from the South China Sea. To hear the weathermen talk, you would think that the whole country was about to sink and disappear. They said that typhoon Yoling, with winds of three hundred kilometers per hour, would hit Manila in twenty-four hours. After three days, she was still nowhere in sight.

In a final act of desperation, I said a special prayer to Jesus just before going to bed. *Dear, Sweet Jesus, Could you please make sure that Yoling gets here by tomorrow. I really don't feel like going to school. But don't make it too strong, please. I don't want the poor to suffer because of me.*

The next day, the first thing I did when I woke up was to run to my window. All I saw were raindrops streaking across the

24

window and dark clouds clinging to the skies. As I changed into my school uniform, a deejay on the radio interrupted a Stevie Wonder song to say, "Don't forget to buy candles and toilet paper. Better save water." While I was putting on my patent leather shoes, he was there again. "Stay dry, my loves. Don't forget your umbrellas."

Shortly afterward, the driver dropped me off at the Academy of the Sacred Heart, where I was in the sixth grade. No sooner had I walked into the classroom than a sudden crash rocked the building. Yoling had arrived. She was slamming herself against the limestone walls, hurtling back and forth, grunting with the ferocity of a caged tiger. I heard the wind shudder through the narrow passages between buildings, softly sobbing in counterpoint.

At morning recess, Janine, Cecilia, Connie, and I were engrossed in a game of jackstones. We were sitting with our legs crossed, our knees carefully covered by the pleats of our skirts. We didn't want to attract the attention of the nuns, who were always sneaking around with their wooden rulers, making sure that our modesty was never compromised. But the only man who ever came to visit us was the priest who said mass. He wore dentures and was half-deaf and partially blind.

I was playing my turn, an intricate routine, when Janine said suddenly, "My daddy saw your daddy last night." I didn't like Janine. We played together only because she was Cecilia's friend and Cecilia was my best friend, and because Janine's desk and mine were next to each other in row five, so whenever the recess bell rang there was really no way for me to avoid her.

Now, I ignored her. I had been playing nonstop and was on my third round. Today's winner would receive caramel popcorn and the latest poster of John Travolta.

"Where?" asked Cecilia.

"Hey, Viola, don't you want to know where?" Janine persisted. I continued on to my fourth round.

"So tell us!" demanded Connie.

Janine put her hands on her hips and said loudly, "My daddy saw Viola's daddy checking into the Hyatt Hotel with a woman. My daddy said it wasn't Viola's mom."

Cecilia and Connie were quiet, but I knew they were looking at me. I felt the weight of Janine's triumphant smile.

"What was your daddy doing at the Hyatt, Janine?" asked Cecilia.

"How do you know it was Viola's daddy?" Connie demanded.

"Because my daddy said so," Janine said. "My daddy doesn't lie."

I leaned against my heels and rocked back and forth, looking at Janine.

"So?" I said, narrowing my eyes.

"So? Your daddy was with another woman, and all you can say is 'So!' " she taunted. From the corner of my eye I saw more students edge closer to our group.

"Liar! My daddy and I were watching *Mork and Mindy* last night."

I lied. I had gone to my parents' bedroom and found my mother alone in bed. She shrugged when I asked her where Daddy was. My father didn't come home that evening.

"Shut up!" Cecilia yelled in my defense.

But Janine was unstoppable. "Viola's daddy has a girlfriend! Viola's daddy has a girlfriend!" she chanted, jumping around me.

I closed my eyes and covered my ears, wishing Janine would evaporate. The harder I pressed my hands against my head, the more her voice came at me like a million burning arrows piercing all at once. In the background I heard Cecilia, or maybe Connie, say, "Leave Viola alone or I'll call Mother Concordia!"

I felt a numbness creep to my toes. My body was hot, and my armpits were drenched in sweat. Everything I touched seemed to stick: the cold marble floor, the wiry lace trimming on my socks, the stiff starch in my blouse. Even my skirt began to feel like second skin. I stood up, and the jackstones landed on the floor, emitting soft, tiny *pings*.

"Janine, look at what you've done to Viola!" Connie shrieked. We all stood there frozen, as if we were in a game of statues.

"Viola's made a number one! Viola's made a weewee!" someone outside our group shouted.

I looked behind me and reached back to my skirt. It was a wet, shiny gloss and it reeked of stale urine. I let go of my skirt and saw a dark red imprint on the palm of my hand. I brought it close to my face, the intensity of the smell shooting straight to my head. Then I felt something on my legs, and when I looked down, I saw a thin line in the same dark red crawling toward my socks. As I turned around to run, I heard Connie say, "Viola's got her period."

I ran so fast the world around me became a blur. I had no idea where I was going, only as far away as possible. Somewhere behind me I heard the bell ring. Recess was over, but I knew I was not going back to the classroom. I continued to run despite the walls towering high above me, their rusty iron spokes banishing all thoughts of escape. Then, just when I thought that my heart was going to explode, I saw our school chapel, its heavy, wooden doors quaking in the storm. I climbed the steps and pushed them open.

The chapel was empty except for the red candles burning on the altar. The nuns had just finished their afternoon Benediction and left a trail of incense in their wake. I hated the smell of incense, but at this moment, I couldn't have enough of it.

I walked to the middle part and took a pew next to the sculpture of the *Pietà*. As I carefully fixed my skirt so as not to disgrace the house of God, I saw my blood and remembered where I was. I began to cry. I cried because I was cold; because Yoling came a day too late; because I got my period. The nerve of it, to come in front of my friends! Without warning! How could I have lost my poise in front of so many people? My mother was always telling me never to show my emotions because it meant weakness.

"People can take advantage of you. Don't ever cry in front of rich folk. Never make them think you're not one of them," she said, her voice revealing the many tears she had shed in the quiet privacy of her heart. "Emotions are only for the weak and foolish."

I guess I am not my mother. I had never felt so small and foolish in my life.

The Academy of the Sacred Heart was an all-girl Catholic school with a reputation for accepting only the daughters of Manila's elite. Students from the provinces had to make do with a waiting list unless they were fortunate enough to have well-connected Manila relatives. It was at this school that the de la Rosas, de la Cruzes, and *de* this and *de* that received their education. Not even the very rich Chinese Dees could enroll at the Academy because their *dee* was not the right *de*.

Our school had several Spanish nuns imported from the main convent house in Barcelona. The *tisays,* as we called them, were crusty-looking women draped in gray and cream-colored habits, their beady eyes following us wherever we sat. Our Mother Superior, an elderly creature who always looked constipated, was quick to rear her veiled head like a cobra to hiss at anyone who sang out of tune or too loudly during services.

Most of the students didn't like the *tisays* because they were always sniffing around with their thin, bony noses, barely able to speak English or Tagalog. My friends and I once secretly held a small mirror to their hems to find out just what made them so superior to the rest of us, and found nothing but the matching gray bloomers they all wore.

My family was not *that* rich, but because my father gave the school a hefty discount on books and supplies—and always published the high school yearbook for free—I was accepted as a student. My parents were thrilled when they received the acceptance, and to celebrate, my father decided to take the family out for a Szechuan dinner in a new restaurant. "No Chinatown dim sum for my baby," he said proudly.

It was only long after I had left the school that I discovered the restaurant belonged to a sister of one of my father's girlfriends. No wonder my mother was so glum throughout the meal. No wonder she hardly touched the food and kept glaring at me each time I helped myself to more of anything.

It never bothered me that there was no *de* in my name and that I didn't come to school in a Benz, a Lincoln Continental, or some other flashy imported car. At least I got to school in a chauffeur-driven car, accompanied by my *yaya* Charing, who was always impeccable in her pink gingham uniform and white shoes. I was only too thankful that I didn't have to use public transportation while the rest of my classmates were driven in their sleek cars. And I always got an A in handwriting.

We Academicians were known for our unique penmanship. Day after day, an hour at a time, we were forced through the hard labor of handwriting exercises, looping our *L*s and *D*s so that they opened just so, making our *M*s and *N*s slope sharply to the right, our *V*s and *W*s evenly and elegantly zigzagging across the page. On paper, our penmanship looked like interconnected cathedral spires reaching up to the sky, taking its place next to heaven, a shorthand to God.

Our penmanship was our school's single most distinguished contribution to our education. It set us apart from the other girls' schools, who dismissed our handwriting as pretentious and our ability to marry wealthy husbands as elitist.

"Viola, are you all right?"

It was Mother Concordia, my homeroom teacher, whom we always called Mother Corny behind her back because she told us jokes that only she could laugh at. I nodded as she sat next to me, placing a gentle hand on my shoulder.

"Janine—" was all I could say, and she understood.

"Cecilia told me."

I remembered my skirt and started to pull away, afraid of soiling her habit. She took my hand firmly in hers and said, "It's all right. You don't have to be ashamed. These things happen all the time. Even to me. Didn't your mother tell you?"

I shook my head, and she sighed. "She probably didn't think it would happen so soon," she said.

"Janine was lying," I said. "I hate Janine!"

A frown crossed Mother Concordia's forehead. She put her arms around me and said, "Sshh, we musn't have hate in our hearts. Remember what Jesus told us? We must have only love and forgiveness. Even for our enemies."

She pulled me down to kneel, and together we recited two Our Fathers, two Hail Marys, and two Glory Be's. We also said a special intention for the Holy Father. I had raised my right hand to cross myself when she suddenly added another special intention for my family, murmuring something about "strength and togetherness." Then she stood and said, "Let's go to the clinic."

I followed her as she walked quickly into the rain, her rosary beads rattling against her hip. At the clinic, she approached the nurse on duty and said something to her in a low voice. The nurse smiled knowingly. Mother Concordia turned to me and said, "You'll be fine now, Viola. Nurse Gloria will take care of you. Just stay here for the rest of the afternoon until it's time to go home. God bless!"

I stood in the middle of the clinic, unsure of what to do. Nurse Gloria moved about cheerily, humming a song as she went from one task to the next. When she was done, she turned to me with a smile. She was holding a white garter loop with two plastic oval hooks dangling on either end. On one hook was a thick wad of cotton wrapped in gauze. I had never seen such a contraption before. In the nurse's other hand was an extra plaid skirt and a pair of underwear. In heavily accented English, she said, *"Dis is a gartur velt. And her is your sanitary nafkin. You fut it tru dis and full. Den you do da same to da udder side. Now, her, let me see you do it."*

I took the belt, skirt, and underwear and locked myself in the bathroom, pulled down the toilet seat cover, and sat staring at the plastic shower curtain with its iridescent polka-dot design. The smell of freshly applied disinfectant stung my eyes. I was angry now at my mother. She hadn't prepared me for any of this. I removed my skirt. My white cotton half-slip was stained. I removed my panties and looked at the tiny globs of blood that had gathered around my crotch. Before I got dressed, I bent over and looked to see if the blood was still flowing. All I saw were traces on the outer rim. So this was what periods were like: They were gross. I changed quickly and came out. Nurse Gloria was sitting by her desk, smiling again.

"Was it deepicolt? How do you peel?"

"I feel like there's a pillow between my legs," I said.

"You'll be *pine*," she said. She invited me to come near her and began to point at a plastic model of a female body's "flumbing sistim." I wasn't interested. I just wanted to go home. Despite what Mother Concordia had said, I couldn't get Janine out of my mind. I had no intention of letting her get away so easily.

At 3:30, Nurse Gloria handed me a paper bag for my soiled belongings and said that I could leave. I walked out of the clinic with my head bent low, afraid to look up and catch someone's inquiring eyes. But no one was looking. As I approached the front drive, I saw my mother standing by the open door of our powder blue sedan. Next to her was Mother Concordia, their heads bent toward each other.

"Viola! Viola! Don't forget your things." It was Cecilia. She ran up to me with my jackstones in her hand, carrying my school bag and lunch box.

My mother was standing alone by the time I joined her. I greeted her with a kiss and asked, "Where's *yaya?*" but she only stood on one side to let me in.

We rode home to the steady rhythm of the windshield wipers and the sound of floodwaters lapping against the sides of the car. Through the window I saw men running with their pants rolled up to their knees, and women daintily holding up their skirts with one hand, carefully balancing a crying child with the other. A few cars were stalled on the street shoulder, while others plodded along, shiny outriggers approaching a shore at low tide.

Our driver had his body pressed close to the steering wheel, mumbling to himself, angry at having to drive in this weather. Our car suddenly jerked to a stop, and the curse that had been dangling from his lips finally broke free.

"*Putangina,*" he cursed in crisp, clear syllables. "That sonof-a*vitch* almost killed us!"

"Eladio!" my mother said sharply.

She strongly disapproved of cursing; she said it was the language of servants, the lower class, and the uneducated. But she never complained when my father said "Shit!" or "Gothamit!"—perhaps because they were in English—although I cannot erase the sting of her hand from my cheek the first time I used the word *fuck* around her. Eladio murmured an apology, bowed his head closer to the wheel, and drove on.

As our car pulled into the driveway, I saw that my father's gold Toyota Sprinter was already there. I got out of the car before Eladio turned off the ignition and headed for my father's den. When I pushed the door open, I saw him walking around with his eyes closed, lost in Rachmaninoff's Second Piano Concerto. He turned around just as the piano solo came to an end, but before he could pull me into his arms, I shouted, "I wish George Hamilton was here instead of you!" and ran to my bedroom.

As I changed from my uniform into my house clothes, my mother came and sat by the foot of my bed. "Do you want to talk?" she asked tentatively. "It's all right. Mother Concordia told me."

She got up and started walking around my room, fingering each sharpened pencil and uncapped pen that stood on my holder, then my closet door where posters of The Bee Gees and John Travolta were thumbtacked next to each other, and finally to my dresser, where a picture of my parents and me was taped on the mirror's hand-carved wooden frame.

"I'm sorry you had to find out this way. I was going to tell you when you were a little older, but I guess"—she stopped and smiled—"here we are." She took two short steps closer to the bed and stood by the edge. "Don't hate your father. He loves you very much. This thing is between your father and me. But I'm afraid that we won't be hearing or seeing the last of his women, so you better toughen yourself. When you've been

33

married this long, you learn to stop asking why. Today it's one woman, tomorrow another. What matters is that he doesn't leave us. We can always put up with the rest."

She came over and cupped my face between her hands, "But remember this: When your turn comes, don't you *ever* pay the same price."

I wasn't interested in what was going on between my parents. I had other things on my mind. Janine was going to get it.

My mother and I were sitting on my bed, her hand gently stroking the top of my head, the way she always did when I was younger. I had almost forgotten how soft her hand was. I kept my head low, counting her pedicured toes over and over again. Then she stood up abruptly. She turned to ask me if I wanted to join them for dinner. When I shook my head, she said she'd have a tray sent up instead. As she was leaving, I remembered something and called out to her, "I got my period." But she didn't hear me and closed the door behind her.

●

7

You didn't think that I would notice. You didn't think that I would see. But I did. Because I do not see merely with my eyes, but with a vision that begins from the heart, transmitting pulses to the brain, triggering responses that are beyond the probing reach of reason. You didn't know that, did you? I know you better than you think. In the same way that I knew that you were lying, I also knew that you were leaving.

It was the last Sunday in May, a time when fading afternoons and slow crimson sunsets precede the silent passage of summer. We had just returned from a *Flores de Mayo* procession in our neighborhood.

You've always said that processions were a waste of time because all anyone ever did was walk for blocks on end and create traffic jams. You didn't like the idea of holding a burning candle and having its wax drip all over your gold and carnelian pinkie ring. But who were you fooling? The real reason you didn't like processions was because you couldn't stand walking behind old women and being forced to sing the *Dios Te Salve* with them. You said that they all looked like the *impactas* and *multos* who inhabited your nightmares, the countless aunts and

35

godmothers who smothered you with hugs and betel-nut kisses at family gatherings.

But this *Flores de Mayo* was different. Mom had been chosen by the neighborhood association to be this year's grand marshal, the coveted *Hermana Mayor*. She couldn't say no. You wouldn't let her say no. This was to be your crowning glory!

She had never looked so elegant and so beautiful. So radiant. I remember her gown well. It was a heavily embroidered one that you had ordered specially from the very expensive couture house, Cordero de Manille. The sequins and glass beads blinded everyone who saw them. You were so proud of her. For once your eyes didn't stray. I know. I was watching you the whole time.

I didn't think you were capable of singing the *Dios Te Salve*, but there you were, singing really loudly, as if the Virgin Mary couldn't hear you. As you and I walked alongside the procession, you couldn't stop telling me how I would be like Mom some day. A beauty queen.

Yours was a very small gesture really. You probably didn't realize it. Or didn't care. We had just sat down for dinner: you, Mom, and I. We were all tired from the long day, Mom especially. The table was set as it usually was, and you sat there with me on your right and Mom on your left. For as long as I was old enough to take my place at the table, her place was always to your left, because that led directly to your heart line, you said. As we unfolded our napkins, our maids appeared from the kitchen with a tureen of steaming *sinigang na bangus* fish soup and a platter of chicken and pork *adobo*.

Sinigang and *adobo* were the mainstays of our Sunday dinners. It didn't matter what we ate during the rest of the week so long as we had *sinigang* and *adobo* on Sundays.

When you were a young boy, your mother used to cook the

36

soup in a clay pot because there was something about the way the earth leached into the food that brought out the strong sour flavor. For broth, she used only fresh young tamarind and the first rinse from the uncooked rice, allowing the tamarind to boil and simmer until its dark brown skin peeled away. Then she would scoop the softened pod and squeeze its pulp through a piece of cheesecloth until the muscles in her arms ached, the tamarind juices bursting into delicate puffs of green as they dropped into the water. Then she added the slices of *bangus* fish: the tail, the belly, and the head, cooking them for no more than three minutes. Longer than that, and the flesh begins to flake away.

A crushed *bangus* fish head wasn't worth serving, you always told anyone who cared to listen. I was amused by your obsession with fish heads, but I didn't want to trivialize your feelings. It was only after you told me how, as a child, you were never allowed to have the head because it was always reserved for your father, that I began to understand the fish-head thing.

I felt sorry for you when you told me how you used to watch your father savor each bite, not once offering you a piece, and how, when you tried to sneak one for yourself, your mother slapped your hand and snapped, "You'll have your turn when you have your own house."

So when we did move into our mansion, one of the first things Mom served you was *sinigang na bangus* soup. She decided to go and buy the fish herself, much to the surprise of our cook, who usually did the weekly marketing. This was not going to be some ordinary fish from the neighborhood *talipapa* or the supermarket. For you, she was going to brave Baclaran market, where the largest and freshest seafood could be found. She had never gone before, and I could tell that the thought of venturing there on her own terrified her. She insisted on taking me along, as if I, a lanky nine-year-old, could diminish her terror.

37

When we arrived, we stood by the entrance for a few seconds, bracing ourselves. It was the smell, an intoxicating blend of the salty sea at low tide and the rotten remains of the city sewer at the end of a humid day. I couldn't stand it, but she pulled me in before I could run and make my escape.

"Pflack! Pflack!"

I looked down and saw my white sneakers covered with mud and the scattered entrails of some unfortunate *pompano* that hadn't escaped the cleaver in time.

"Padaan nga, ale, padaan!" a voice grumbled from behind, ordering us to get out of the way. It was an old man with a burlap sack of muddy oysters, all crunched up from the weight on his back. His bare feet looked like freshly dug ginger root. I mumbled an apology and immediately stepped aside as his yellowed eyes locked into mine. Men and women pushed us all at once, forcing me to swallow the air from their stale breaths; the grime from their clothes left its mark on my bare arms.

We went from counter to counter amidst the shouts of zealous vendors eager for a buyer, their fingers skittering in front of our faces, each of them claiming us for their own. Mom searched for the biggest and freshest *bangus* fish lying among the rest of the day's catch, your fish obsession becoming her own. Foot-long mackerels, speckled *lapu-lapu,* ruby red snappers, mussels, prawns, and curious crabs warily eyed the depths below. They glistened against garlands of seaweed, like jewels on soft velvet. Once she found your *bangus,* she haggled for the best price in such a spirited fight that the vendor finally acquiesced in order to get rid of her. It was an inspiring performance, one I had never seen before.

When we returned home, she insisted on cleaning the fish herself, using the serrated edge of a kitchen knife to scrape its thick, stubborn scales, scattering them about in a shower of crystalline flakes. Her hands were cut by the prickly gills and tough jaws, but she held them up to me as if they were rings and bracelets engraved with your name. As she squeezed the tamarind through the cheesecloth, she invoked your mother's memory, her raspy voice whispering, "Harder! Harder! Harder!"

I remember how your eyes sparkled when she put the soup bowl before you, the *bangus* head draped in bright green *kangkong* leaves, lying on its side. You hurriedly picked up the head with your fingers, noisily sucking on the eyeball, chewing the succulent cheeks, slurping the soft flesh of the belly and spitting out a lethal bone. As I sat and watched you, I imagined your father in your place. He was murdered by a rival candidate running for town mayor when you were a law student. Your mother never cooked *sinigang* again, and she died without ever knowing what had become of you.

When you were done, the naked bones arranged neatly like tiny sun's rays around your plate, I waited for your verdict, confident that you would bestow a bouquet of praises on Mom. "That was good," you said, "but not as good as my mother's."

Right then and there, I decided that you didn't deserve my mother.

She was determined to get the next one right, but each time you said, "Not quite." One day she gave up trying and threw the cheesecloth into a heap of rags. You never complained again.

On this particular Sunday, the maids had just served me soup and disappeared into the kitchen when you asked, "Do either of you want the head?" I continued to drink my soup, pretending that I hadn't heard the question. But somewhere inside of me, I felt an odd sensation creeping in.

"What's wrong with it?" Mom asked. "Wasn't it cleaned properly?"

You frowned and looked down at the fish. "Oh, no," you answered. "I'm just not in the mood for it tonight."

"We'll give it to the maids," she said. "Do you want something else?"

"I'll just have the *adobo* for now."

"Are you not feeling well, Dado?" she asked you carefully, trying to keep her voice neutral, hoping to keep me out of the conversation.

You took her hand, patted it lightly, and looked her straight in the eyes, your own never flinching. "No, of course not."

That night, I lay awake in my room, thinking about your marriage. I had always thought these things happened only to the people in Flavia Moravia's gossip column that you and Mom talked about, the ones who were always being condemned by the Church and the Catholic Women's Action Group Against Immorality. Compared to those people, our lives were so ordinary.

I walked over to your door and saw your head buried deep in the pillows, content and childlike in the shadows. It would have been easy to slit your throat at that very moment. Except that there was Mom, her body one with yours. She loved sleeping next to your armpit, finding comfort and solace in its familiar smell. Like overripe bananas, she once said. I couldn't remember. I had stopped sharing your bed six years ago, shortly after my eighth birthday.

I felt the waves of sleep gradually take hold of me, the faint sounds of your slumbers humming back and forth in alternating voices. I waited for my tears to come, but they stayed away, indifferent to my pain.

Who was the woman this time? Someone from the bookstore? A friend of Mom's? A stranger whose favors you paid for? Oh, Dad, one of the maids? The next day I imagined shooting all of them on the spot. At a party or in a restaurant, I watched every woman who looked at you, spoke to you, touched you, to see which of them was the one. How many were there, I wondered. Whenever a call came for you, I would run to the extension, hoping to hear the voice of this unseen other. I wanted to know who Mom was up against, yet I wouldn't have known what to do had I met her—or them—face to face.

Then you began leaving trails. At first I thought you were just being careless. Then I realized you were baiting Mom. You wanted her to confront you with the evidence, to rub the alien handkerchief against the stubble in your face and say, "This isn't mine."

I wasn't going to give you that pleasure. I kept them from her reach, including your *Flores de Mayo* pictures filled with the faces of the *zagalas,* the young beauties in the procession, and none at all of her. I wasn't going to let you demean her, demean me, despite the number of women you began to flaunt publicly, humiliating me before my friends. I decided to wait it out, to see who would outlast the other. Until then I was going to be like the bamboo tree, swaying in every direction, strong and sturdy in the wind. But the truth was, whenever the thought of leaving you occurred to me, I realized that I had nowhere else to go.

And neither did she.

8

My mother has been acting strange lately. Yesterday she returned from a weekend spiritual retreat, one of the many she has been attending, full of high spirits and good cheer. At first I thought she had become a born-again Christian, but I found out that her ebullience had nothing to do with Jesus. It had to do with tea.

A nun at the Convent of Sorrowful Thorns had given her a small pack of dried tea made from the leaves and roots of the comfrey plant, which was supposed to cure falling hair, constipation, memory loss, ulcers, and other minor ailments, and also had the ability, when accompanied by a prayer to Saint Anastacia, patron saint of unhappy marriages and unrequited love, to amend a husband's philandering ways.

My mother was now saying, "We have to make sure that your father drinks this, *without fail,* for nine straight days." The challenge was getting him to drink the tea without letting him know.

"Why do I have to do it? It's not my marriage."

"He's your father."

That was how I ended up brewing the tea. Early in the

morning, long before the maids began their chores, I mixed a proportion of two tablespoons of dried leaves to three cups of water, said the prayer to Saint Anastacia, let it boil for two minutes, and then placed it in the coffee carafe from which, every morning, my father poured himself a cup or two. On the seventh day, when my father abruptly announced that he would be leaving my mother, she flushed the remaining tea leaves down the toilet.

Books like *I'm Okay, You're Okay* and *How to Win Friends and Influence People* began appearing on her night table, replacing her collection of romance novels. I didn't know whether to be happy or sad, but I began to worry for my mother's mental health. I casually asked her where her collection was, and all she did was point me in the direction of the bathroom or the maids. In the past, whenever I caught her reading one of these books, she would immediately hide it under her housedress and pretend that it was never in her hands.

I could not understand the fuss. She said the books were too—I loved her word for it—pornographic for my virgin eyes. I almost choked.

"They're no big deal!" I heard my father say to her once when, for the nth time, she had pleaded with him to stop bringing home *Playboy* and *Oui* magazines. How silly they both were! All I had to do was phone my father's executive secretary and ask her to messenger me the latest issues. Or I could borrow our driver's personal collection, which he had saved from my father's discards.

But now my mother didn't react when I asked about her collection. She didn't even ask why I wanted them. My father became "your father." Marriage forced them to become each other's surrogate parent, the kind one was forced to live with by an accident of birth. I wondered what they had done for sex.

Mom didn't look as if she could tell an orgasm from stomach cramps.

Something inexplicable drew me to their bedroom. It was the best room in the house. My mother had decorated it in soft hues of salmon and lime, filling it with blue-and-white ginger jars from China and Lladro and Steuben figurines. In the middle of the room was a hand-carved four-poster bed where my mother would sometimes lie in the afternoons, enjoying the view of the garden and the floral scents that wafted in. She would lie in this room for days whenever she became depressed over my father, over her failed marriage, over the uncertainty of her life. Sometimes, I could hear her mumble, *"No tiene por donde."* Nowhere to go.

My father was sleeping in their room less and less, preferring the one next to mine whenever he was home. On those nights, I would lie still in the darkness, waiting for him to turn the door-knob. I listened for the sound of his footsteps shuffling softly on the carpet as he made his way to the bed, and the creaks and squeaks of the springs when he finally lay down. Then there'd be a pause, followed by a deep sigh. Next I'd hear him turn off the light. Only then would I know for sure that he was really home. Only then would I be able to close my eyes, taking flight into a world inhabited by nuns in colorful native G-strings and virgins having sex orgies with demigods astride a bunting of fluorescent half-moons.

I ran to my father's closet and pulled the doors open. His clothes were still there. I opened his drawers and found his socks and underwear. Still, something didn't feel right. When I went to the bathroom where he kept his toiletries, they were gone. On the sink was an old razor. His terry bathrobe was not to be found; it had been my Christmas present to him. His writing desk was empty, and his favorite portrait of the two of us together at the beach was gone.

"He's gone, isn't he?"

My mother was standing in front of her vanity table, struggling to get into her strapless bra, her hair held back by a headband. Her face was fully made up. She stopped, reached for a tissue, and wiped off the sweat.

"It's over," she said.

In the next breath she told me that his mistress was pregnant with his child, and unless he moved in with her, the woman was threatening him with a scandal. He couldn't afford the public humiliation.

"Why didn't anyone tell me before?" I cried.

"I was waiting for your father to come back from Hong Kong so that we could both tell you." She shrugged. "He and Carol—that's her name—went there to let the gossip die. How considerate of him to leave me to face the music."

"When is he coming back?"

"I don't know."

Of course, I knew about his women. Everyone in Manila did. He was no different from every Filipino male, rich or poor, who had at least one mistress, sometimes two at a time. Nobody ever protested. Not even the Church, which was more concerned about preaching against birth control and the evils of divorce. "We all have our crosses to bear," the priests always said. My mother's marriage happened to be hers.

And now he had left my mother. Without him, she would be nothing and her life would be empty. Where did that leave me? I was not going to be the center of her attention. I was not going to be a scapegoat.

"What's going to happen to us now? Do we have to leave this house?" I demanded.

"No. Your father left us this house. However, he also offered me a lump sum in exchange for any claim to the bookstore and publishing companies."

"We all have a price, after all."

Her hand came to my face so quickly I don't remember seeing it leave her body. The next thing I knew my cheekbones were on fire.

"You better apologize right now, or you'll be grounded for a month!"

"You're taking it out on me because he's not around for you to yell at."

"Well, if you must know, Miss Smarty Pants, I didn't take the money. I told him I'd rather die than sign over the company to him."

"So are you getting anything at all?"

"Nothing. Nothing whatsoever," my mother said quietly.

"But he has to pay!"

She looked at me and said, her voice soft and weary, "I want to be left alone. You don't know what you're talking about."

For the next three days, my mother and I didn't speak to each other. She would be in the hallway just as I was opening my bedroom door, and I would slam it shut. At dinnertime, she'd send for a tray, or leave the table as soon as I walked in. Once we even backed into our rooms at the same time as soon as we caught sight of each other.

This lasted until the day I happened to answer the phone. It was my father.

"Darling!"

"Daddy! Are you back? Where are you? Why didn't you tell me?"

"Look, I just got in from the airport, and now I'm in Dasmariñas. We'll talk later. I need to speak to Mom."

Dasmariñas. He got his wish after all. He was living among the half-breeds. I didn't know he already spoke their language.

"Will I see you?"

"Any time. Mom knows where to reach me."

I knocked on her door and said, "Phone. Daddy."

"Thank you."

Later that night, she came into my room and said, "He's having all his things picked up tomorrow. He said that you should visit any time you want. Sleep over even."

Live with him maybe, I thought, but then felt ashamed by it. Whose side was I on? I didn't even know Carol. My mother stood very still. I was sitting on my bed, and I continued to watch her. Finally, I got up and put my arms around her.

"Was I such a bad wife, Viola? Was I really *that* bad?"

I gently pulled her to the bed and sat her down. She lay on her side with her knees tucked in tight against her stomach, her clenched fist pushed into her mouth. Her entire body shook.

It embarrassed me to see her this way, but I couldn't bring myself to say anything to her. I reached down and began to stroke her forehead, slowly working my fingers into the tangled mess of her lacquered hair. Left, right, front, back, my hands went, parting each strand, smoothing the tiny wrinkles that had gathered in her forehead, wiping the tears between her nose and cheeks.

"Do you still love him?" I asked.

"With all the bile in my body."

That night, my mother and I slept in the same bed. Mine.

9

"Who's Divina Magtanggol?" I asked my mother as I handed her an airmail envelope postmarked from the United States. It was the third letter she had received from the same person in the past month.

"A pen pal?" I teased.

My mother snatched the envelope without giving me an answer, tore it open, and removed three sheets of paper covered with long, oval pen strokes. She looked up at me and smiled. "Divina Magtanggol was my best friend. She, Chinggay Valencia, and I all went to the same college. The three of us were like sisters. Back then we were inseparable."

"Why haven't I met them?"

"Because they don't live here anymore. They live in the U.S., though I haven't heard from Chinggay in a while. Dede—that's short for Divina—left Manila shortly after her father threw her out of his house."

"That wasn't very nice."

"He found out that Dede was seeing a married man who turned out to be his best friend. What an awful time that was. I couldn't even invite her to live with us, because my father, your *lolo,* didn't approve. He even wanted me to break off our relationship."

"So she went to the States."

"Not right away. First Chinggay and I found her a convent for women in her situation. Then she left just the same. She's never come back. Not even when her father died. We've kept in touch off and on. Birthdays, Christmas cards, exchanged pictures."

"Is she married?"

"She's never mentioned a husband in any of her letters."

"Does she know about you and—?"

"Yes." My mother handed me Dede's letter to read.

"Dear Ludy," it began. *"I can't tell you how much I'm looking forward to your arrival."* Here I looked at my mother, who told me to read on.

It's been a long time. I'm glad you've finally decided to come. You should be thankful that your good-for-nothing husband has finally left you! Let somebody else suffer his cruelty. We'll have all the time to talk once you get here. First things first.

There are a few things you need to know in order to make your trip a success. Be wary about accepting letters or packages from friends and relatives in Manila who may ask you to deliver them to some aunt in Staten Island, or a Mr. Nacanaynay in the hinterlands of Minnesota. If an immigration officer finds you suspicious—it may be the way you clip your hair, the pin on your lapel or just the smell of your perfume—they can ask to open the packages or your purse, and there's nothing you can do to stop them.

Don't give these people any reason to keep you out. But I know how it is: Filipinos don't understand the meaning of no. If you must, insist on reading the letter or examining the contents of the package. Anything that might compromise your trip, no matter how insignificant, should be returned. Or burn them when no one is around. You can always claim later on that your baggage got lost.

Avoid landing in Seattle and Honolulu; these are the worst ports of entry because they are always watching out for potential illegal aliens. If possible, fly directly to New York. Once you land at the airport, take your time getting to the immigration booths. The immigration officer you end up with will determine your successful entry into this country. Avoid blacks. They're jealous of Asians. Whites are safer; they just want to leave at five, down a six-pack, and watch TV.

Males are preferable, the older the better. Treat them like your lolo *but don't overdo it! What you want is to cross that yellow line as quickly and smoothly as possible.*

Don't draw attention to yourself. Don't smile too much: They can tell if you're hiding something or not. Look naive but not stupid. Look them straight in the eyes but never in arrogance. Keep your answers simple. They're well trained at picking out inconsistencies in your story.

With luck, it will all be routine, and you'll get your six months right away. Be calm. Don't ever show them you're afraid. It's a good idea to have some loose change in case you need to make a phone call. If something happens, God forbid, call this number; they'll know where to find me. Don't bring this letter with you, not even on the plane. In the worst case scenario, I will deny everything.

Love, Dede

When I was done, I looked up. My mother had left the room. My hands were wet and shaking. My parents were running away from me. I couldn't believe they were actually running away from me.

. . .

"So you're going to America," I said to my mother several days later, trying to sound matter-of-fact. We were at the perfume counters in Rustan's, shopping for a fragrance that would match the Cordero gown I was wearing for my high school senior prom in two months.

"I have to, or else I'll die," she said with a tone of finality in her voice.

"When did you decide this?"

My mother lifted her shoulders and merely looked at me.

"For how long?" I asked impatiently and immediately felt foolish because I knew that this trip wasn't going to be just a vacation.

"I'm going to live in America. I'm going to try to work there." Her lips widened into a smile as if she had just seen an apparition of the Virgin Mary.

"Doing what? You've never worked in your life!"

"I used to work when my father was still alive. Before your father stepped in and told me to—oh, never mind."

"But you're not a citizen."

"There are ways—" Her voice drifted farther and farther away.

"Where will you live? You won't have money! You won't have maids! You won't have a driver!"

You won't have me.

"I could start all over again. I could always sell my jewelry and live off that."

"Why does it have to be America? It's so far. You'll end up sounding funny."

"Manila will never let me forget that I am still Mrs. Diosdado Dacanay," my mother said.

"What's wrong with that? You are."

"And so is that Carol who has the gall to refer to herself as Mrs. Dacanay. Who knows how many more out there are calling themselves by that name? Look, this place has become too small for your father and me. My friends think it was my fault your father left. They said I should have learned to look the other way. I couldn't even get a bank loan to open up my own business because I would need your father's signature as a guarantor. Nobody wants to hire me. Do you know what your godfather did when I went to see him for legal advice? He took me to a very nice restaurant at the Intercontinental Hotel, and over coffee he casually mentioned that he had re-served a deluxe suite on the sixteenth floor. Can you believe that? Your own *ninong.*"

"Are you going to get a divorce?"

"You're asking too many questions. I just need to get out. Now!"

"So go to Hong Kong!"

"Stop it, Viola! You're getting on my nerves."

"Then stay!"

My mother put down the bottle of Joy and abruptly walked to another counter. She had a beautiful neck, but at that moment all I could think of was squeezing it between my hands. With sudden urgency, she began spraying herself with many fragrances all at once, filling the small space we were in with the heady smell of a funeral parlor. Then she stopped just as suddenly and walked back to me.

"Come with me," she said, holding out her hand as if we could fly away at that instant. Who did she think she was? Peter Pan? *What about my prom?*

"Let's go to New York and live there," she said. "My God, Viola, we'll have so much fun. Let's leave this rotten place. Your father can have Manila all to himself. They can all rot together!"

She laughed out loud, and people began to stop and stare at her. I moved away, refusing to take her hand; I was afraid that if I did, we would both drown. I didn't want the curse of her birth to become mine.

"I thought so," she said and headed for the exit. I paid for my Shalimar and ran after her.

The day of her departure came a month and a half later. Four of us took her to the airport: her friend Girlie, who cried throughout the ride; Girlie's husband, Porcing; and their driver. My mother insisted on keeping her departure a secret. In this, the final act of her marriage, she wanted to make a dignified exit. She was taking two large, very full Louis Vuitton suitcases and one matching carry-on tote bag. She had packed them as if her life could fit into each of its different compartments, careful not to waste space, snapping the locks shut so that nothing else would escape. She was traveling first class.

As the car struggled up the airport drive, we saw the departure area was jammed with people, most of them there to say good-bye. They came by the truckload, traveling from remote towns, enduring hours of travel along dirt roads to wave farewell to a brother, a best friend, a wife, a neighbor. They were drawn to the airport by the vicarious excitement that travel held for them, or by the unspoken fear that every good-bye might be a final one. Long after the passengers had gone through the arched gate of the metal detector, the well-wishers continued to linger, to hold for just one more moment the sight of a disappearing head or a waving hand.

When we finally got to the departure area, we all jumped out of the car, each of us taking something to carry. I felt bodies rub against mine. My mother had her hand on my shoulder, her mouth shouting last-minute instructions. I could hardly hear what she was saying, overwhelmed as I was by the throng in front of me. The next thing I knew, it was time for her to go. She hurriedly kissed her friend and her friend's husband, quickly nodded her thanks to the driver, embraced me tightly.

Early that morning, my mother had taken me aside while the maids finished the packing for her. "You're going to be running this house now. I'm depending on you to take care of it," she said to me as I felt the tears welling up in my eyes. In a conspiratorial tone, she added that we were not to cry in public. "You know how I hate scenes," she had said, her contact lenses filling with delicate beads of water.

Now she was gone. She didn't even turn around for a last wave. I stayed on the spot she had just left until I could no longer see the gold buttons on the cuffs of her navy-blue blazer. I whispered, "Good-bye," and left.

On the way home, *Tita* Girlie tried her best to cheer me up. She said I could live with them for a while if the house was too big and empty. She'd be sure to come visit every day. "It's going to be hard for the first few days," she said kindly. Then she asked what my plans were. Would I live with my father? Or rent the house and move to a condominium?

All I really wanted to do was drown myself in self-pity. I was relieved when we finally arrived at my house. *My house.* I must get used to calling it that. Perhaps not having my parents around wouldn't be so bad. I ran to my mother's bedroom, locked myself in, and closed my eyes. Perhaps she hadn't left. Perhaps she was just watching TV or putting on makeup. But when I finally opened my eyes, I knew that I was truly alone.

Her bed was a mess, and the shoes and clothes she had left behind were strewn all over the floor. The drawers of her night table were wide open. One by one, I picked through her things, afraid of what I might find, wary of painful truths they might reveal. I found the old portfolio case that my father had used when he was still a student. The one he was carrying the day he first met my mother. It now appeared to have been freshly slashed many times over. I found a folder full of newspaper clippings with photographs of my father's girlfriends, their young and attractive faces marred by fangs and raccoon eyes. I tore them to shreds and threw them in the trash can.

That night I slept on her bed, wearing the nightgown she had worn the night before. The smell of her perfume was everywhere, lingering in the bed sheets, the drapes, the carpet, her gown's cotton lace. Next to my skin it was as if she was there, warm and alive. As I lay wondering where in the Pacific her plane might be, I felt strange. This was the bed my parents and I used to share. I remembered always feeling safe and secure between them. I was taller now, and with all this room and them not here, I felt vulnerable, afraid.

My father kept calling on the phone, wanting to speak to me, but I told *yaya* to say that I had gone to bed early. I knew what he was up to. He needed a dumping ground for his guilt. I wished I could hate my father. It was he who got us all into this mess. But hating him was too obvious. Too easy. I decided to hate America instead. If it weren't there, my mother wouldn't have left. She'd still be here lying next to me. It was better for me to kill every memory I had of my mother.

I didn't want the burden of missing her.

10

Eight days after my mother left, I received a letter from her. It arrived the day after the prom. I wondered if she had timed it that way.

My fingers trembled as I held it in my hands. I didn't open it right away. I felt around the envelope, measuring its thickness, guessing how long her letter was, its length a measure of her love and longing for me. I liked the way she wrote my name. *Ms. Viola Dacanay.* The *Ms.* made me feel worldly. When I write her, I must not forget to mention that since her departure, the maids have begun calling me *Ma'am* Viola. In her absence, they consider me the mistress of the house.

As I tore the envelope open, the name on the return address caught my eye: Lourdes Sanvictores. Only eight days since she left, and she had already reverted to her maiden name. To a life before my father. She certainly got over him quickly. I was still sorting out the mess the two of them left behind.

I never realized how small my mother's handwriting was until I saw this letter, the words flowing in graceful lines and loops like fine lace. Her letter consisted of three sheets of yellow pad, filled front and back. *Dearest Viola,* it began. The first paragraph was a *how-are-you-I'm-fine* sort of routine. She asked about my prom. *Did I have a good time? Hope I didn't stay out too late. Didn't drink too much. Send her a picture.* I could tell that even from a distance she intended to retain parental control over my life.

The rest of her letter was far more interesting. She talked about her flight and how empty the first class section was. How the food was terrible. How she could barely eat. How she couldn't stop crying.

> *I almost thought of turning back. What was I doing on this plane when I should be there with you? Maybe coming to America was not such a smart idea after all. If I just learned to ignore your father and his women, Manila wouldn't seem so intolerable. It occurred to me that I didn't know anyone in New York except Dede, and what if she turned out to be different from the person I used to know?*

I skipped a few sentences, my eyes eagerly scanning the part that might say when she was coming back. I looked up and down, back and forth, but I didn't find anything. Not even a hint.

> *—and the immigration was a breeze. Of course, the officer asked me all sorts of questions. He even asked where your father was, since my passport said I was a housewife. I was quick with my answer. I said he was baby-sitting. The man thought that was funny. Of course I knew better, but he didn't have to know that! He gave me six months. Thank God for novenas. The other humorous incident occurred at the customs inspection area. I was told to open up my luggage, which I found odd, since I*

had nothing to declare. But the next thing I knew, this man, this complete stranger, was digging into my belongings. My God, he was black no less! Viola, he touched my panties and bras!"

Here I giggled. I found her melodrama excessive. It wasn't as if they were on her when he inspected them!

And adding insult to injury, he asked me if I had any fresh mangoes. Apparently, Filipinos sneak them in all the time. As if I would put them in my Louis Vuittons. He probably doesn't know a fake one from the genuine thing.

She was glad to be with Dede, she wrote. It turned out that her initial apprehension about her friend was totally misplaced. Dede's apartment was somewhere in Long Island City. That's not the same as Long Island, my mother pointed out. Long Island was where a lot of rich people lived, like the Forbes Park of the Philippines. She said that if people asked where she was staying, I should simply say Long Island. Let *them* figure out the difference. For now she will be Dede's house guest until she can find her own place.

I've never been on my own, Viola. I feel so different about myself. So this is what it's like to be unmarried and unattached. I could get used to this. Imagine: your mother, a single, swinging New Yorker. I tell you, Viola, I can't breathe enough nice, American air.

Toward the end, she gave me Dede's telephone number and address. She warned me that until she found a job, she might not be able to afford long-distance calls. Letters would have to do.

When I finished reading her letter, I noticed that the paper was wet. I also noticed that my fingers were stained with ink. I don't remember when the first teardrops fell. I don't remember how long I cried. Nowhere in her letter did she mention how much she missed me. How much she wanted me.

Nowhere.

11

I dream about you again. We are in a small boat tumbling through the rapids of a river, our bodies undulating with the rise and fall of every wave. I cannot tell if anyone else is with us because you and I are in front, you directly behind me. It is a humid day and the trees lean over the embankment, forming a protective canopy as we go along, shielding us from the sun. We do not have umbrellas, and the wind stole our hats long before our journey began.

You are shouting at me to keep my hands out of the water. I had lowered them into the river, allowing them to trail us as our banca snaked its way around the large boulders. I am fascinated by the sight of my hands becoming distorted as they comb the water's metallic surface, tendrils wrapping themselves around each of my fingers.

You do not see it that way. You keep pulling at my hands because you say that the water is dirty. That animals bathe themselves in the water. I ignore you, even when you say that the river mermaid will take me away. You think that will frighten me. I am braver than you think. I have never seen a river mermaid. I can hardly wait to meet one.

Then, suddenly, the river is transformed into a bubbling bed of hot lava that threatens to melt the boat. I hear frantic voices shouting as arms and bodies reach over my head to scamper for safety. We are pushed toward a waterfall just as our boat begins to hover over the edge. I feel a pair of arms lift me onto dry land. I turn around to pull you with me, but I am too late. The lava has swallowed you. There is no trace of the boat. All gone. I cry and cry.

From a distance, I hear a voice shout my name. I think it is your voice and come looking for you. "Viola! Viola!" the voice says, and I say, "I am coming! Wait!" I open my eyes quickly and see someone else. It is only yaya. *She is telling me that Daddy is on the phone.*

For weeks after my mother's departure, I was deluged with visits and calls from every uncle, aunt, and cousin in my family. I received invitations for dinner, for a beach outing, and once, *tita* Girlie even offered to take me to Hong Kong for a weekend of shopping but I declined. Pots of food arrived so frequently, my dining table began to resemble a banquet for twenty. But more than the food, I would often come home to find plain white envelopes bulging with cash waiting for me. I set these aside for my mother in case she ever needed the money. For some reason, she never did.

My father insisted that I move in with him in Dasmariñas. That meant, of course, moving in with Carol and their newborn son, whom they named after my father. My father argued that it was improper for a young lady like myself to live alone in a big house. It did not matter that the house, in my mother's absence, was now mine. Or that no one would actually think that I was the mistress of a rich sugar daddy. My father was afraid that my reputation would be harmed by my living situation.

"It is not right for you to live alone. People will say you're too liberated. What will they think of our family?"

I found his overnight conversion to moralist hypocritical and annoying. I did not answer. Perhaps he would go away. But he was persistent. And persuasive.

"Look," he pleaded, "maybe we can still be a family" and, as my eyes widened in horror, he added hurriedly, "Let me make it up to you. Remember how, as a little girl, you wanted a brother? Now you have Jake. You have so much to teach him, Viola."

I told him that it was a little too late for me to play older sister. He replied, "And Carol really isn't all that bad."

Neither was Cruella De Vil.

I agreed on condition that it would be for only a month. I wanted to check out Dasmariñas for myself, to see what the big deal was all about. My father was profuse in his gratitude for what he thought was his second chance. I suddenly began to have second thoughts, but it was too late to back out.

On the day I was to move in, Carol showed up at school, holding an armful of gladiolas. I thought she was going to make an offering at the chapel, but the flowers, it turned out, were for me. She was dressed in the brightest of fuschia suits with matching shoes and handbag. I remembered seeing that suit somewhere. Of course! It was my mother's. Carol's nails were long and lethal, her perfume suffocating. I decided she was a wasteland of bad taste.

I was eager to get into the car, taking her along with me, but she wanted to be seen. Without asking and before I could stop her she blithely introduced herself as "Carol Dacanay" to Mother Concordia, who sneezed as soon as she came close. Through Carol's chatter, Mother Concordia nodded politely, inviting her to attend afternoon prayers and join her for coffee afterward. Carol quickly apologized and said it was time for us to leave.

As soon as we got to their house, I knew that I wouldn't make it through the first week. Everything about the house was triple deluxe gaudy. The bedroom she had decorated especially for me was wallpapered with pink cabbage roses the size of her head, and pink curtains as billowy as parachutes. There were pink balloons everywhere, each stamped, "Welcome, Viola!" On a different occasion I might have been moved by her graciousness, but today I wished I was in my own room, my own house.

I missed my mother.

That night, at our first meal together, Carol regaled my father with the story of how she had made a big impression in my school. As big as an asteroid landing on my head, I thought. She assured my father that she and I were going to have a great time together. My toes curled underneath the table. My father was grinning from ear to ear, buying into the Walton Family scenario she was presenting to him. Then he pushed his plate away and disappeared into his study, claiming that she and I needed to indulge in "girl talk."

Over the next few days, I could tell that the family bit my father had hoped for was not working. I knew that he knew it too, but he chose to ignore it, still hopeful that it would somehow resolve itself. He insisted that we should all sit down together for our evening meals, but Carol complained that she didn't want to miss *Knots Landing*. On another occasion, when my father came home with the news that he was thinking of launching a weekly women's magazine, Carol yawned and excused herself, claiming that she had dysmenorrhea. I looked at my father. He looked like a fallen hero. Perhaps it would have been better if I hadn't seen any of this, if I had no reason to compare what he had lost with what he got in return.

The night my father was at a business dinner, Carol and I were halfway through our meal when, without any prompting on my part, she decided to give me her analysis of exactly what had happened between my parents.

"You know, Vi," she began, using Vi as if we were on the most intimate of terms, "just as it takes two to make a marriage, it also takes two to end one. Don't blame your father."

Next, for sure, she was going to tell me that she was also not to blame. I began to feel the pounding inside my head getting stronger and stronger. I excused myself and went to my room to pack my things. It didn't take long—I hadn't brought much with me.

I was waiting in the living room when my father came home. Carol, I assumed, was watching TV. He didn't act surprised when he saw my suitcases. His relief was palpable: It was as if he knew it would end up this way. He offered to drive me home. We didn't talk much. He pulled up at the front of my house and got out to remove my stuff from the trunk. He had just put my bags down on the curb when I went to give him a good-bye kiss. The gesture surprised him, but he didn't step away. We held each other for a long time. In his arms, I thought I could almost love him again.

When we separated, I could see that he was crying, loud, shameless tears, and mumbling, shaking his head, and tightly embracing himself. I leaned closer to hear what he was saying, but he shrank away from me. Seeing him like this, I could not imagine how two people could be so different from each other and still decide that marriage was where they ought to be. I could not believe that there was ever a time when my parents truly loved each other.

"Did you marry Mom because she was pregnant with me?"

I stood there, waiting for his reply: a denial, an explanation—something, anything that would give me the benefit of my doubt.

My father straightened up and wiped his nose and eyes with the back of his hand. He planted a kiss on my forehead, got into his car, and drove off. There was nothing left for me to doubt anymore.

12

As mistress of this house, I have made a list of ten requirements for a smooth, orderly summer:

Number 1: Wake up no earlier than 11:00 in the morning.

Number 2: Go to sleep no earlier than midnight.

Number 3: Have breakfast in bed (garlic fried rice, pork *longganiza,* sliced tomatoes sprinkled with salt, fresh fruit in season).

Number 4: Wait for Cecilia to call.

Number 5: Call Cecilia.

Number 6: Hang out at the Polo Club, especially at the racquetball and squash courts, where *mestizos* are never in short supply. (I could never understand why they preferred these sports over tennis or swimming. Maybe they just didn't want the sun to get on their pale white skin.)

Number 7: Convince a *mestizo* to pay for my club check.

Number 8: If Number 7 fails, DO NOT PANIC! Proceed to Ayala Avenue for the weekly anti-Marcos protest rallies—I just know I'll find lots of *mestizos* there! I must be sure to wear my *yellow* T-shirt with the face of the slain hero, Ninoy Aquino, Jr. (Since his death, *yellow* has become the color of protest.) Also my *yellow* socks, *yellow* sun visor, and my *yellow* fan. I'll ask *yaya* to prepare for me and my friends two sacks full of *yellow* confetti (toilet paper and the *yellow* pages of the phone book should do it) and have Eladio haul them to the fifteenth floor of the Pacific Building, where, at three o'clock in the afternoon, we and other protesters will bathe the entire Avenue in *yellow* rain. I'm so excited!

Number 9: If Number 8 fails, organize a singalong party.

Number 10: At the end of the summer, go to college and get an education.

Buhay baboy. It's a pig's life.

Ever since Cecilia returned from Los Angeles, where she and her family spent three weeks traveling and shopping, I noticed how her behavior had changed in ways that didn't agree with me. Not that any of this would alter our relationship—we were best friends, after all—except that in the course of her trip, she had brought back new habits that I found strange and irritating.

So what else is new? was one of her new phrases, matched by an equally irritating attitude. She uttered the words with a breezy nonchalance totally inconsistent with the kind and caring person I'd always known her to be. When I had the mumps in the seventh grade, she made me a humongous get-well card signed by our entire class. On the card's front cover was Cecilia's interpretation of me and my illness—a blowfish with bobbed hair and cheeks the size of basketballs. I still have the card.

She also began wearing makeup, her puckered lips brimming

with lipstick and generous applications of Johnson's Baby Oil that constantly ran beyond her natural lip line. Seeing how genuinely captivated she was by her appearance, I didn't have the heart to tell her that one needed sunglasses to look at her. Or to be seen with her.

This new side to Cecilia needed some getting used to. In the past, whenever she and I spent our Saturday afternoons roaming around Rustan's department store, we always stopped at the cosmetic counters to sneer at the matrons who submitted themselves to the beauty experts for what seemed to be hours of beauty consultation.

The experts buffed their skins with a chalky solution, scrubbing as hard as they could, while the women winced in their seats. The solution was actually a skin whitener that promised a complexion as fair as Snow White's. The ads even went as far as to show Snow White sitting before her vanity table, applying the stuff to her face, the mirror before her reflecting the anticipated whiter, fairer skin.

When my mother was still around, she used to nag me to use those skin whiteners, as if they were supposed to correct what nature had overlooked. I could never understand her preoccupation with my skin color; it wasn't as if I was spotted or anything like that. It wasn't as if she was bleach white either. But her obsession stood between us. Despite my strict adherence to the solution, my complexion never changed. It remained as brown as the *chico* fruit. My mother eventually gave up and stopped buying it for me. "Oh well," she sighed, "your exotic looks will land you a foreigner for a husband." I guessed that if I couldn't be Snow White, I might as well be a Bird of Paradise.

Cecilia and I could not stay away from the matrons, sitting stiff and still, their skin sweating under the bright spotlights. There was so much plaster on their faces that every time they moved, soft flakes fell on their clothes, dotting their collars and sleeves with specks of ivory powder. Once, unable to control ourselves, Cecilia and I looked at each other, blurted "Never!" and ran away laughing.

But of all the things Cecilia brought back with her from her trip, her constant use of the word *shit* bothered me the most. *"Shet!"*

"Cecilia, it isn't like you were in America for ten years. You were there for only three weeks, for heaven's sake, and now you've come back talking like you were born there!"

"Oh, Vio," she said lazily, "unless you speak like them, you'll never be understood."

"Who's *them*?"

"The *kanos,* the Americans, who else? One day, my mom and I were walking around Rodeo Drive and decided to check out the Giorgio Armani boutique. I went to one of the racks and pulled out a T-shirt. Next thing I knew, a salesclerk was breathing down my neck, trying to take the shirt away from me. I asked her if it was one hundred percent cotton. She didn't hear me the first time, so I said it again. You know what she did?"

Here Cecilia pinched her nose and said in her best American twang, "'Hundred percent WHAT?' And I said, 'Cotton. Is this one hundred percent cotton?' Then she smiled and said, 'Oh you mean *kuhtn.* Well, it certainly is.' When I asked her if I could try it on, she snapped that it was two hundred fifty dollars. The nerve of the bitch! Did we look poor? My mom was carrying her Hermès bag. She held the shirt up to the woman's face and said, 'That's all? I want ten of them in different colors. And make sure they're extra small, because Filipinas are not as big-boned as you are.' The woman staggered toward the storage room looking completely flustered. Serves her right for trying to mess around with my mother. As we were leaving, my mom said to the store manager, 'You'll hear from the Philippine government about this!' Viola, I was so proud of my mother."

"She was only a salesgirl, Ces. You're home now, so you can get rid of your *kuhtn*. If you continue talking like that, nobody in Manila will understand you."

"Oh, don't be such a spoilsport. I'm sure even you wouldn't mind speaking with a twang."

"Not if it makes me sound like a goat."

At that point I decided it was in my best interest not to discuss anything serious with Cecilia until she got over her bout of Americanitis.

13

onths have passed since my mother's departure. During that time, I have received several letters from her. They usually arrive every other week on a Monday. Her letters are actually note cards, the kind that have reproductions of artworks by Van Gogh, Matisse, and Picasso and are sold by the box at the Metropolitan Museum of Art for $8.95.

They usually don't say much. The last greeting was the one I loved best: *My child.* I noticed that she rotated her salutations so that she never used the same one consecutively. Her lead paragraph was always the same: *How are you? I'm fine. What's new?* They always sounded as if she was having a conversation with herself. From there she proceeded to enumerate the things that had happened to her between the time she sent her last letter and the one I just received.

Dede doesn't want me to leave. She insists that I stay with her until I get my bearings, find a steady job, save enough money, or one of us gets tired of the other. Good news! I finally saw Chinggay after all these years. The three of us had a fab—that's short for fabulous—dinner reunion in Chinatown. Dede whis-

pered to me that it looked like Chinggay had a nose job, but we shouldn't say anything.

Got my social security card. Ditto for a New York driver's license. It's not bad driving an automatic—like having an Eladio who doesn't talk back. It feels good to be around another Filipino. Dede has no room for feeling homesick or lonely. I'm still looking for a sponsor. I'll eventually find my own place. Hate subways. Oh, if only Eladio were around.

She wrote in these spare, telegraphic sentences as if longer ones would suffer in transmission or convey more than she wanted to reveal. She was careful not to repeat the same story twice, giving me the date of a previous letter for cross reference. I suspected that the reason she used note cards and an occasional aerogram was so that she could always say that she was running out of space or room or paper or something to that effect. Not only did her letters come in neat, compact sizes, she went out of her way to send me the same cards for my own use. I never used them. I was not bound by her sense of space. They're sitting somewhere in my closet waiting to be recycled for the next birthday party I'm invited to.

Our phone conversations were no different. They came sporadically and lasted no longer than a spurt. The first time we spoke on the phone, I was so stunned I couldn't speak. She thought we had been disconnected and almost hung up on me. When we did speak, her voice sounded nervous, even unsteady. Or perhaps that was what I wanted to believe. I don't remember what we talked about. It was enough to hear her voice across the ocean and above the time zones.

In another conversation she said that she might have found a place, a midtown dormitory for women run by Carmelite sisters.

How she could live in a place like that after living in our mansion escaped me.

"Do you get your own bathroom?"

"It's not the Waldorf, you know," she snapped.

"Who are the other people in the dorm?"

"It's popular among Filipinos."

I reminded her that she'd probably come across one or two who might have known her in Manila, and if not, the new acquaintances she would have made would waste no time gossiping about her and asking how much money she had in the bank. Several days later I got a card from her saying that she had given up her reservation at the dormitory. She claimed that she had only recently found out that they had a 9:00 P.M. curfew.

The last time we spoke she told me that she had just bought herself a bookshelf for her future apartment, wherever and whenever that may be. She emphasized the word *whenever* as if I was getting in the way of her independence. I pretended not to notice and continued to listen. Her voice was tired, and she was short of breath.

"Can you imagine your mother hauling this gigantic box up four flights of stairs? I almost broke my back!"

I was amused by her sense of accomplishment, as if she had just figured out a way to preserve the ozone layer. We were having an almost good time over the phone. I told her about the new friends I was making at the De La Salle University where I was a college freshman, the *mestizos* at the Polo Club, Carol and how she was driving Daddy crazy with her social climbing— Mom really loved that one! About how we would someday spend Christmas together.

My mother suddenly went all cold.

"Listen, this call is getting expensive," she cut me short. "I'll call you in two weeks. Same day, same time. Love you." *Click.*

She forgot that I was paying for the call. Sometimes, I didn't know why I bothered.

My father invited me to spend the Christmas holidays with him and his family. He seemed to have forgotten the results of our last attempt at getting together. I told him that I had already made plans. Cecilia and her family had invited me to join them at their country villa in the mountains of Baguio City. My father didn't force me. He said to call him when I got back.

I lied. It's true that Cecilia had invited me, and I had said yes. But at the last minute, I changed my mind and said I'd stay behind. Before she left, she warned me not to commit suicide. I wondered why she said that.

This was going to be my first Christmas alone, and I thought that if I could survive this one, I could survive anything. In late November I began putting up the Christmas lights and hung the paper lantern with the star motif by our front door. I brought out all of my mother's Christmas decor: the foot-high angels with trumpets, the dozen or so gilded reindeer that she scattered all over the living room, the Christmas balls she always placed inside one of her Waterford bowls, the wreaths that hung on our windows, the evergreen garlands that framed every door in our house. And, of course, the Christmas tree.

It was not a fresh tree. Its branches were plastic, and the pine needles were made of very fine wire painted green. We'd had this tree for as long as I can remember. My mother always took charge of decorating it. When I was old enough not to break anything, she allowed me to help her. My father's role was to place the star at the top. No matter how many transformations our lives went through, no matter that we saw less and less of my father, that ritual remained unchanged. It was one of the few constants in my life that I was grateful for.

As I hung each ball and strung one lightbulb after the next,

I kept praying for strength to get through this. When I placed the Nativity scene under the tree, I felt that, yes, I would survive this holiday without suffering any serious emotional mishaps.

By mid-December I was in full swing, at Rustan's every day, shopping for no one in particular, but going through the motions just the same. The next nine days, I attended the *misa de gallo,* the dawn masses that lead up to the midnight mass on Christmas Eve. Each night, before going to bed, I set the alarm for 3:30 in the morning and got up just in time to brush my teeth, change into sweat pants, and run the five blocks from my house to the church. I loved walking home afterward, surrounded by others like me, watching the sun as it came up slowly over the rooftops, and having a breakfast of hot cocoa and rice cakes that the old ladies sold at the church grounds.

I had never attended these masses before. My mother always did. I was too lazy to get up, too drowsy to sit through an hour-long mass. I thought that going to church on Sundays was enough for me. I was pretty sure that I was in good standing with the authorities up above.

On Christmas Eve, I was so excited I got to church earlier than usual. I managed to find the last remaining seat in the front row, right under the lectern where the priest would deliver his sermon. For this service, the chorale was accompanied by a pianist and a string quartet. As the mass got under way, I was so completely lost in the pageantry that I didn't notice the priest coming our way in his traditional greeting of "Peace Be with You." As I watched him come closer to me, I found myself getting choked up, my voice unable to rise from my lungs. The priest was now standing before me, and as he said, "Peace be with you and Merry Christmas," I bent my head low as rivulets of tears formed pools around my feet.

I ran out shortly after. I had been terribly wrong. There was no way I could survive another Christmas like this. One never got over being left alone. One just got used to it. The next morning, on Christmas Day, I stayed in bed watching, over and over, a tape of *It's a Wonderful Life.*

All day.

14

One day, I was on my way home from school when Eladio handed me a note from my father. He wanted to see me for a private dinner and discuss something important. *Private* was code for *without Carol.* I hoped he wasn't going to try to talk me into bonding with her. I admired him for wanting to give it another shot, but she was his mistress, after all.

Eladio dropped me off at the La Primavera restaurant, where my father was already sitting at his usual corner table. He offered me a position in the bookstore. "Only part-time," he added quickly, "and nothing that would interfere with school." He thought it was good for me to understand the business rather than just sit around the house, and, he said very, very carefully, "pining for your mother."

Startled, I looked at him. How dare he try to assume what I was thinking! For the first time, I became aware of him *as a man.* Not as the man who called from time to time to ask how college was coming along, or the man who scolded me for overspending at the Polo Club, or the man who gave me tips on acing a tennis serve. I was seeing my father as a man with the kind of urges that got him into trouble with my mother.

I stripped him of every vestige of parenthood and looked at him with the cold detachment of someone unrelated. What did *they* see in my father? How could anyone be willing to excuse certain realities about him? What did my mother ever see in him? It wasn't money. Back then, my father had no money to speak of.

I remembered something my mother once said about my father's looks: "Your father was not a handsome man." She told me this long after all three of us had recovered from the George Hamilton–James Brown episode, long after the need always to make excuses for my father's shortcomings had left her. I was touched by her apology, though I had not asked for it. After all these years she was finally able to summon enough courage to acknowledge what was in plain view, and in doing so admit to herself that her marriage was not meant to be. "He wasn't very tall, he was slight of build, and his skin was almost as dull as pewter. I think the reason my father hired him was because he didn't have to worry about Dado making a pass at me. Well, I proved my father wrong!"

"Did you know that I actually *seduced* your father?" She smiled mischievously. "Back then I still had a sense of humor, and I was feeling particularly reckless. Don't laugh. It's true. The first time I saw your father, I thought his eyes were going to swallow me whole. They were dark and deep-set and they looked back at me with the intensity of a full moon. I knew I had to have him. Your father accepted me unconditionally, and for the first time I felt I could do no wrong. He wasn't an ordinary houseboy. He was a working student. He was studying to be a lawyer. He was making plans for Yale or Harvard. Imagine that, Viola, you might have been born in America. Can you imagine how our lives would have turned out if that had happened? But your grandfather died, and with him went our future. I don't remember exactly when your father began to change, but I remember the lying. I've never felt the same about myself again."

I looked at my father now as his knife sliced his filet mignon. His face was full of concentration.

"Was it something that *she* did?"

He looked up at me with a frown. "Who, she? Who are we talking about?"

"Mom. Why all the women?"

Very carefully he put down his knife and fork and dabbed his lips with a napkin. Then he put his elbows on the table and leaned on them, making a clicking sound with his tongue as the last bite went down his throat.

"Marriage is complicated," he said.

"How complicated can it be? You marry one person, you stay with that person, and that's it." I felt bold; I didn't want to lose my momentum.

"If only it were that simple. People change. I changed. Your mother changed. You must believe me when I say that I had no intentions of leaving your mother—"

"Except that you got Carol pregnant!"

"Except that Carol got pregnant."

Just like you got my mother pregnant.

We continued to eat our meal, limiting our conversation to something safe and familiar. I told him that I wasn't interested in menial work like cleaning bathrooms or emptying trash cans. "That wasn't what I had in mind for you," he replied, sounding defensive. "I'd like to think that you're going to be part of the management. All this will be yours some day. I expect you to know how to run it."

He assigned me to the flagship store in Makati. Three times a week, from ten in the morning until six at night, I was a salesgirl in the Romance section, dispensing advice on the latest bestseller or naming the author with the most vivid love scenes. I hated the work. I didn't like acting as a love counsel to women who had no love life to speak of, other than the ones they read about from cover to cover, devouring each word and each line as if it held the secret to a happy ending. Their unhappiness reminded me too much of my mother.

Unfortunately, I couldn't ask for a transfer. That was a rule my father and I had agreed upon before I took on my assignment. I was not going to be entitled to any special treatment because I was his daughter. My identity was kept confidential. My paycheck came directly from him.

In the beginning I thought my father was using me as his watchdog. I did not disappoint him. No one ever suspected that he and I were related. I warned my friends never to come to the store on the days that I worked, and the driver always dropped me off four blocks away. The closest that anyone ever came to asking me something personal was when they wanted to know where I went to school because obviously I was not of their kind. I lied and gave them the name of an obscure college, crossing my fingers and hoping that nobody else had gone there.

My disguise was so thorough and successful that the other employees gossiped freely about my father's new girlfriend. One of them even pointed her out as "Sir's latest chick." I guess I would have been amused by it all had the girl not been that much older than me. She was certainly a lot younger than Carol, and prettier, but in a cheap sort of way, and she couldn't put together a straight sentence in English. It was hard enough dealing with my father as a womanizer. Did he have to be a dirty old man as well?

15

Shortly before I reached my seventeenth birthday, I made an important discovery: My life was boring. I had no vices, no illicit activities that I could gleefully indulge in away from the prying eyes of my parents. Cigarettes gave me asthma, alcohol made me drowsy, and marijuana, despite what everyone said, was simply overrated. I couldn't brag about a sex life because I needed to have one in the first place. Without a boyfriend, I didn't see how that could happen.

So I did what any young woman in my situation would do. I joined a religious organization. I was not terribly religious, although I went to church every Sunday and never failed to light a candle for a Saturday night date, or say the appropriate novena prayers for a passing grade in calculus. I joined an organization because Cecilia was already a member, and according to her it was a great way to meet guys. "Think of it as church-sanctioned dating," she assured me.

It was called the Circle of Saint Ansegisus, and the only really religious thing about it was its name. The Circle, as it was called for short, was one of several organizations under the auspices of the Saint Ansegisus Catholic church, a wealthy parish community in Makati. While I didn't live there, I had friends who did and could vouch for my good breeding.

Father Patrick Philip, an American from Illinois, was the church's parish priest and the Circle's spiritual adviser. Everyone called him Father PP. He wore Levi's and Birkenstock sandals under his brown cassock robes, and he also cursed a lot, "Satan's bastards!" being his favorite. He never cursed around the matrons, who could have had him deported back to Peoria on a moment's notice, and he always made a sign of the cross immediately after as a form of instant absolution.

Our group met on Saturday nights in one of the church's meeting rooms. We sat around in a circle like the Apostles waiting for the Holy Spirit. After a short prayer, our leader would begin a group discussion on either a passage from the Bible or a saint whose life might be an example for us in these modern times. This would be followed by a progress report on the group's various civic projects and future fund-raising activities, like a bake sale, a craft fair, or a scavenger hunt for Halloween. We concluded our meeting by rising, holding hands, and bowing our heads to recite "The Lord's Prayer."

It was a strange way to spend a Saturday night when everyone else our age was either at the Firehouse Bar, dancing at the Counterpoint Disco House, or having a good time at one of those love motels. Having been to the Firehouse and Counterpoint many times before, I thought it was time to try something new. So when one of our regular meetings ended early, I suggested that we head out to Pasig, a suburb considered to be the capital of motel country. When the guys began hooting with excitement, I said, "Sorry. No boys allowed!"

"What!?" they all shrieked.

"I would never dare bring any of you along!" I added, heady

with the authority that came with being the group's vice president for internal affairs.

I turned to the seven women in the room and asked who wanted to come. Cecilia, naturally, was the first to raise her hand, followed by Candy Montecillo and Libeth Illusorio, who eagerly volunteered her Range Rover as our means of transportation and her husband, Jerome, as our chauffeur. The three other women hurriedly excused themselves, and as they were rushing out I overheard one of them mutter something about lighting a candle for our souls.

As the five of us piled into the silver Rover, Candy asked, "Which one are we going to?"

"The Tropicana," Libeth said.

"Yes, ma'am," he replied, tipping an imaginary cap at her and driving away.

"You've been there?" Candy asked. At thirty-three, she was probably the oldest in our group and, I suspected, though it had never been confirmed, a virgin.

Libeth nodded sweetly. "We went there a lot before we got married. Wouldn't it be nice if it was still the same, honey?"

"You mean, you weren't a—" Cecilia asked carefully.

"No one ever is. This is the twentieth century, after all."

"Did it hurt?" Candy asked.

Jerome snorted as Libeth playfully swatted him in the arm.

It was a fifteen-minute drive to Pasig, which, besides the motels, was known for its factories. Jerome made a right turn from Epifanio de los Santos Avenue, called EDSA, and headed directly onto Ortigas Avenue extension, where billboard signs introduced us to Pasig's salacious side.

"Orchid, just fifty meters ahead!" screamed Cecilia.

"Champaca, loveseats galore! Orchid II, we always have room for you!" read Candy.

"NO BLACKOUTS! FREE SLIPPERS! FULLY AIR-CONDITIONED! CABLE TV!" yelled Jerome. Pasig had to be the Las Vegas of motel country.

"That's it! That's it!" Libeth pointed excitedly to her left as the Tropicana loomed ahead.

Except for her and Jerome, the rest of us were dumbstruck. The Tropicana was more Sleeping Beauty's Castle than sex palace, and at any moment we expected to see Mickey Mouse making a grand appearance before us. There were parapets, towers, a drawbridge, and medieval stained-glass windows. At the center was a waterfall, illuminated by colored lights timed to flash with the background disco music. At the bottom of the waterfall was a small wading pool where several children from the nearby slum were now thrashing playfully.

Jerome stopped by the entrance just as a taxi was pulling out of the driveway. We all leaned over to see who was inside, but it was only a white man with his pickup for the night. When they left, a young man jumped in front of us, waving at Jerome to follow him inside. We got to a checkpoint where a security guard walked up to the driver's side and another man went around peering through the windows. With all the antigovernment protesters going around and rumors of the rebel group, New People's Army, swarming into the city, they wanted to make sure that we were neither. How many rebels drove around in a Range Rover?

From where we were parked, we got a glimpse of the motel and were mildly surprised by how plain and homely it seemed. It looked like an apartment complex composed of two-story row houses, painted white. There were thirty or so units up ahead. Car after car pulled in and out of garage doors as young men in white uniforms scurried across the driveway, balancing towers of newly laundered towels on their shoulders and carrying plastic buckets filled with scrubbing brushes and cleansers.

As Jerome opened his window slightly to speak to the check-in clerk, Cecilia, Candy, and I quickly crouched into the leather upholstery to hide our faces. Libeth did not join us. She sat up proudly with her back straight and her head high.

"Good evening, sir."

"Boss, *may* vacancy *ba*?" Jerome asked.

The clerk must have thought that Jerome was some sort of sex loony, a lone male with four women. We didn't hear the rest of their conversation because it was drowned by the Harley-Davidson pulling up behind us. After Jerome closed his window, a room boy appeared and pointed us in the direction of a garage door. When we got there, the roomboy pulled the door open, walked inside to switch on the orange lightbulb, and turned around to guide the Rover in. As Jerome came close to the wall, the room boy slammed a hand on the front fender, shouted, "Hhepp!" and sprinted up the short flight of stairs where, we assumed, the room was. He ran down again, said, "It's ready," and closed the door behind him as he left.

Only then did Jerome cut the engine. He turned to us with an impish grin and said, "Welcome to the Tropicana, girls!"

Libeth was the first out of the car, and she was up the stairs before any of us had even opened our doors. By the time we caught up with her, she was lying on the water bed, her hips swaying left and right, lost in the wave of her memories. Jerome took it upon himself to be our tour guide, explaining that the Tropicana was popular for its theme rooms. The one we were in recreated Neptune's underwater castle, or at least that's what it looked like to me. There were all sorts of sea creatures and vegetation that seemed more appropriate to a sci-fi movie than a room where sex was supposed to take place. But when Jerome pressed another switch, the images were suddenly suffused with a neon glow, transforming the room into something magical and erotic.

On the bedside console were several control buttons. When Candy touched one of them, the sound of waves lapping against the shore and gurgling water bubbles filled the room. We all giggled except Jerome and Libeth, who were holding each other's hands, their eyes closed, probably plotting a way to get rid of us.

In front of the bed was a clear glass panel where we could see the shower room. Cecilia was there now, waving at us to join her. She pointed at several water spigots rising from the floor and jutting out of the walls, each pointing in a different direction. "I guess they want to make sure that every orifice in your body is clean," she observed.

When we went back to the bedroom, Libeth was perched on a monstrous-looking contraption that resembled a praying mantis. It had an elongated seat wrapped in leatherette, two pairs of metal legs for support, a pair of arms extending from either side of the body, and a pair of footrests on one end.

"I never saw this before," she said, twisting her body this way and that, trying to figure out how it worked.

"It's a love seat," Jerome said flatly.

"For what?" Candy asked.

"You're supposed to do it there," he replied. Candy gasped and immediately left the room, crossing herself many times over.

I ran my fingers along the cold, metallic arms and legs and took my turn on the seat, my rear end not quite able to find a comfortable resting place.

"You'd have to have some muscle control to *do* anything in this one," I said.

"Whoever thought of it had quite an imagination," Cecilia remarked.

"Hmm, you seem to be knowledgeable, Jerome," Libeth said, but in her hazel eyes I could detect a glint of her famous temper.

"Juanito described it to me," Jerome said, suddenly looking flustered.

Libeth stood in front of her husband with her hands on her hips. "Don't drag our poor driver into this, Jerome Illusorio!"

"It's the truth," he said, his voice quivering.

"Oh, let's not get so serious," I interrupted. "So this is it. I thought motels had more to offer."

"Let's see what's on TV!" Cecilia said.

"Hold it!" Libeth cried. "The TV's extra." She promptly picked up the phone and ordered the operator to turn it on.

A few seconds later, the screen flickered to life with what appeared to be an old movie. As the fuzz and scratches disappeared, we saw a Filipino couple lying on top of a table, their partially naked bodies wriggling like a pair of earthworms. They were inside a grass hut. We all fell silent and inched closer to the TV set. I saw Candy standing by the door, her face frozen.

On closer view, I could see that the man was actually straddling the woman, vigorously pumping her body. There was nothing sexy about the act; he looked like he was reviving her from unconsciousness. The woman, on the other hand, was wearing a *kimona* and *patadyong*, the native embroidered blouse and skirt that provincial maidens traditionally wore. The camerawork was crude and the cutaway shots were distracting. There was a cut to a rice field with a carabao idly eating grass; a close-up of the woman's fingers gripping the man's fleshy back, her nails manicured and painted in red.

Did people really grunt and snort that much? Then the man slumped over the woman's shoulders and sighed. The screen became fuzzy again and turned black.

"But I didn't get to see the pe—!" Candy complained, just as Libeth threw a pillow at her.

"So much for Pasig," Jerome said, taking a deep, long breath. "Let's go to the Pen Lobby. All that fuc—, I mean, driving has made me hungry." He picked up the phone to ask for our bill, and when that was paid, he herded us back into the Rover.

As Jerome slowly backed out of the garage, we suddenly heard tires screech to a stop behind us. Jerome slammed on the brakes and yelled, "*Tarantado!* That idiot almost caused an accident." He looked at his rearview mirror, preparing to challenge the other driver to a fight, when suddenly he cried, "Shit! Viola, it's your dad!"

This time everyone screamed and hit the floor for the second time that night. Not me. I wanted to see who my father was with this time. As Jerome quickly shifted into gear, I turned to look at my father, who had his hands on the steering wheel. Thank God he couldn't see us. From the way his lips were moving I could tell he was hurling a stream of invectives. I looked at his companion. It was Preciosa Advincula. Cecilia's mother.

"Which slut was your dad with this time?" Cecilia giggled.

I could not answer. As Jerome sped away, I stuck my head out the window and threw up.

16

My dear Viola,

I've just added a new term to my vocabulary. TNT. The Filipino code for an illegal alien. Tago ng tago. Always hiding. Always running. I became one the day my visitor's visa expired. I remember the day well. It was the day I married your father.

The last of my options had shriveled away. I had nowhere else to go, so I stayed. The days were filled with endless visions of being sucked into a deep, dark hole where no one would ever find me. I ceased to exist on paper, a nonentity living on borrowed time. I came to exist only in my own mind.

The transition was easy to make. Yesterday's tourist, today's TNT. No big deal. I learned to substitute one form of life for another and adjusted to it. This was role-playing, just like Manila. From happily married woman to disgraced socialite. But this was going to be better now: I was the lead star. No more playing second lead to the Carols of the world. I was going to give my best performance yet. Academy-award caliber. Quick, hand me my Oscar.

For the first time I could be anything I wanted and when

I wanted. I could take my life anywhere. Any time. My life became a series of inventions, each one better than the last. Spin a win!

Manila was never, could never be, like this. There were too many rules, too much guilt. I got tired of apologizing for things I had never done, for thoughts I had never thought. I got tired of your father. Of carrying a burden of guilt simply because I was born with original sin. Because I was born a girl. The absence of accountability was refreshing.

I never thought I could do it. As I surveyed all that was before me—the wide-open horizon, the turquoise sky—I could smell the air, its sweet purity sweeping through my nostrils, coaxing each and every pore of my being back to life. What was before me was mine. All of it. No one was going to take any of it away from me.

I lied about my status for the first time at a job interview with Flescher and Simmons, a small graphics-design firm on 18th Street and Fifth Avenue. On the day of my interview I wore a pink blouse and a gray suit. I read somewhere that pink was the color of calm and harmony.

"Can you work?" *asked the personnel manager.*

This was the moment I was waiting for. I had rehearsed this scene so many times, I could do it in my sleep. I was so good I believed everything I said.

"Of course. I'm a citizen."

The world did not collapse around me. I was not struck by lightning. Good riddance to guilt and remorse!

When the woman asked for proof, I was ready for that too. My fingers burrowed deep into my handbag, searching for something I knew wasn't there. I took my time, waiting for my hands to stop shaking. "Damn!" *I said.* "I thought I had my passport with me." The manager's lips drooped in disappointment, but I rebounded before she got away.

"But," I said, smiling, "I do have my Social Security card and a driver's license." I showed her a "card" that I had bought for $500 through a friend of Dede's. She assured me that the card was legit—that's short for legitimate—that her friend had never gotten others into trouble.

The manager didn't want the card. Not even when I held it up for closer scrutiny. It was enough that I had flashed my blue Social Security card before her. I could have held a library card in my hand, and she still wouldn't have had anything to do with it.

She told me to report in three days.

Oh, Viola. What a trip this has turned out to be!

Your Mom

17

"Why do you always look up at the full moon, Vi?" Cecilia asked.

Because I was born on a full moon. Because my mother liked full moons, and every time one came around, she'd get giddy with excitement. I can always look at the full moon and know that she is doing exactly the same. Then it doesn't feel as if she's so far away, but as if we're just sitting across from each other, looking into each other's face, touching each other's heart.

That's what I wanted to say, but of course I didn't. Instead I replied, "Because it reminds me of your flat ass!" and we both broke into unladylike laughter.

Cecilia and I were sitting at the poolside of Connie's Forbes Park colonial-style mansion, built at great expense to resemble Tara in the movie *Gone With the Wind*. A formal banquet was going on in honor of Connie's older sister, Sylvia, who was getting married tomorrow. The *despedida de soltera* to bid farewell to her single life turned out to be quite a sendoff. It was an evening affair complete with a twelve-piece orchestra, food catered by the Manila Peninsula hotel, flowers by Ronnie's, and waiters dressed in white gloves and tuxedoes. The entire garden was lit with *capiz* shell lanterns and party lights that hung from the branches of the banyan trees. Life-size plastic swans were filled with fresh flowers and floated on the Olympic-size swimming pool.

I had never seen so many richly dressed men and women. Jewels sparkled and competed with the sky. Everyone who mattered in Manila society was here—including, it was rumored, the First Couple, who was expected to arrive at any moment.

Gossip columnist Flavia Moravia had billed the forthcoming nuptials as "*The* Wedding of the Year," a headline we all thought an exaggeration since it was only the month of January. But Flavia's style was all flamboyant pronouncements, no matter how ridiculously inaccurate they turned out to be. The last society wedding she trumpeted reduced even Prince Charles and Lady Di's to nothing more than an outdoor picnic, British style.

There were at least three hundred gathered here for the first wedding in Connie's immediate family. If Flavia's estimates were correct, the number expected for tomorrow's ceremony would be at least five times that. The only places that could comfortably hold that many people were the Santa Ana Race Tracks or the airport runway, neither of which would be considered socially appropriate. So they settled for the Manila Cathedral for the church ceremony and the whole of Fort Santiago, which they closed off to the public, for the open-air reception. Connie told us her mother had bought out an entire warehouse of eggs and given it as an offering to St. Claire for good weather.

From where we sat, we could see Connie busy maneuvering her grandmother's wheelchair, pushing her around like a grocery cart, weaving in and out of tables and chairs to greet guests. At eighty-eight, Doña Loleng was the imperious but beloved matriarch of Connie's family. With her cotton-candy coiffure, her alabaster shoulders wrapped in a heavily embroidered *manton de manille* shawl, she looked every inch the grand dame.

Doña Loleng was the *lola* I never had. After downing several shots of straight tequila, her austere exterior wore down to reveal a capacity for out-cursing even the most zealously macho male. She enjoyed the company of gardeners, drivers, business associates of her son-in-law, and suitors of her granddaughters because she could trade curses with them and exchange dirty jokes with punch lines that put the men to shame. I rarely saw her around women her age. She opined that they were either dead, in comas, or too senile for her jokes.

I once saw Doña Loleng in action, cornering one of Connie's suitors.

"What do men with big dicks eat for breakfast?" she asked her hapless victim. When the young man replied, "I don't know," she grabbed him by his shirt collar and breathed into his face, "I thought so!" She walked away, her hoarse laughter pummeling the man into lasting humiliation. He was never seen or heard from again.

No one ever dared to assume that they could be on equal footing with her. Anyone who did was banished from her presence permanently. People forgave her her ways simply because she was what every common man and woman aspired to be: a *mestiza.* She could trace her heritage back to the Arrabal family of Bobadilla, Spain, although no one in Manila knew exactly where Bobadilla was. While it was strongly suspected that she didn't either, no one ever questioned her.

Her pride was known to turn sour when she talked about how her only daughter had ended up marrying Connie's father, Cosme Pilapil.

"Es indio," was how Doña Loleng constantly referred to her son-in-law, alluding to the fact that he had not one ounce of Caucasian blood in his body, but a short, flat nose, dark skin, and a solid, angular face. Everyone knew that if it hadn't been

for Connie's father, the Arrabal-Pilapil clan would have had no mansion on McKinley Road in Forbes Park, no collection of European cars on the driveway, no private island off the province of Mindoro that came with its own runway. If not for Cosme Pilapil, Doña Loleng would have been just another tragic figure living a marginal life in Manila society—a *mestiza* with no money.

Cosme Pilapil had made his money in polyester. My father was always making fun of him as The Polyester King of the Philippines, but I knew that behind the mockery, he could barely conceal his envy.

Cosme was one of the privileged few who played golf with the president and could count on him to be a godfather at a son's or daughter's wedding. Connie confided to us that in the coming November presidential election between Marcos and Corazon Aquino, her father was contributing a huge amount of money to the president. In exchange, Cosme Pilapil expected liberal tax exemptions in import duty.

My father resented the fact that he was not part of that circle. He was, I suspected, annoyed that Connie and I were good friends. Once he even asked me to use my friendship with her to get him closer to her father. But I pretended that I had no idea what he was talking about.

"Sylvia's certainly not showing," I told Cecilia after Connie again disappeared from our view.

"Jeez, Vi, what a thing to say!" she replied.

From the covered tennis courts of the Polo Club to the gymnasium of the De La Salle, where Sylvia Pilapil was a college senior, she was known as the Number One Paka, as in *pakawala,* boy crazy. She was getting married tomorrow because she was two months pregnant, a fact that no one dared mention publicly. Right now, people were more interested in professing admiration over how Sylvia had snagged the scion of a steel magnate's family, whose father was, coincidentally, another presidential crony. The marriage had been hurriedly arranged before arithmetic caught up with her physical appearance, and before the reclusive groom could change his mind and escape to some undisclosed location in America.

"Well, do you see anything?" I asked.

"Of course not, silly! It only starts to show in the second trimester," Cecilia said.

"How do you know?"

"Janine said."

"How is she, by the way?"

"Still the same whiny bitch."

We hardly saw Janine anymore. Sometime in our sophomore year she dropped out of school when she became obsessed with an Ateneo student whose picture she had seen in a college yearbook. The idiot got pregnant after one date. Last we heard, she was expecting her second child. Her husband, known as Ting, had quit school to support his family and was now supposedly performing as a bass guitarist in a strip joint in Pasig.

"Oh, look, here comes Connie," Cecilia said. "Hey, Connie, I have a question for you."

"What's that?"

"Who's designing Sylvia's wedding gown?" I cut in before Cecilia could do any more damage.

"Calixto Candelaria," Connie replied, as she sat down between us.

"But he's so old," Cecilia said.

Connie shrugged. "He's a friend of my mother."

"Are you okay, Viola? You look awfully pale."

The three of us looked up and saw Caloy Austria standing there, his face filled with concern. Caloy was a first cousin of

Sylvia's husband-to-be, and the best man. He was an MBA student at Harvard to whom Connie had introduced us earlier, but whom her mother had dragged away before we had a chance to get to know him.

"I'm fine, thank you," I said, distracted by his shiny forehead and receding hairline.

"Do you mind if I join you?"

"Yes!"

"Not at all," Connie and Cecilia replied in chorus.

"Well, which one shall it be, then?" asked Caloy.

"Cecilia and I were just leaving," Connie said hurriedly.

"Oh, right," Cecilia agreed as she stood up and gently shook the grass from her dress. Before they left, Connie turned and winked at me.

I continued to sit by the pool, not having anything smart to say. I suddenly felt naked around Caloy. I could feel his eyes scanning my bare shoulders.

"Do you mind sitting down? It's hard looking up at you," I said.

"I'm sorry." Caloy smiled and sat cross-legged next to me.

He was tall. His legs had to be at least a yard long. He was wearing calfskin shoes with tassels, and I could smell his cologne rising from the heat of his body. From afar, I saw Connie and Cecilia trying to catch my attention, feverishly flashing thumbs-up signs in the air. *The fools!* I wasn't going to give them the pleasure of embarrassing me.

"So," Caloy said, "how are you related to Sylvia and Connie?"

"We're not actually."

"That's too bad. Otherwise, we'd all be one big family. But then, perhaps that's just as well."

I began to chatter. "Connie and I—well, no, actually—Connie, Cecilia, and I go to the same university. We've been friends since we were, gosh, in the third grade."

"How lucky! I can't remember having a friend from that far back."

I looked up to the full moon in time to see soft wafers of clouds glide past it. If only my mother were here, she'd know what to do, what to say. Where were mothers when you needed them?

Caloy smiled. He had nice, even teeth. He held out his hand to me as the band began to play "Spanish Eyes." I put my hand in his, and as I watched his long fingers close over mine, I knew I was going to smile for a long, long time.

Caloy and I were inseparable the whole evening. When I happened to bump into Connie and Cecilia at the powder room, they couldn't stop patting me on the back. "You've hooked him, you lucky girl!"

We were still on the dance floor when the band announced they were playing their last song of the evening. We went over to the bar to get drinks and were just walking back when someone tapped me on the shoulder from behind. It was Honey Parungao, an acquaintance of my mother's, notorious for her big mouth. My mother hated her guts.

"I thought it was you! How are you, *hija*?" She proffered her cheek to me, throwing a side glance at Caloy, who gave a polite bow and stood aside.

"I'm fine, thank you. Nice to see you!"

I half turned toward Caloy to introduce him, but she linked her arm with mine, nodded a curt "Excuse us" to him, and pulled me away.

"*Soooo*, where's your mom? I haven't seen her in a *looong* time. Where's she disappeared to?"

"She's living in New York."

At the mention of New York, Caloy turned toward us, but quickly turned the other way when Honey threw him a sharp look.

"Well, that Ludy!" She sighed deeply. "How dare she disappear like that without the courtesy of a good-bye, and now, not even a letter."

"You know how it is in the States," I said. "She's pretty busy. Even I have to remind her to write me more often."

"You poor thing. You must miss her terribly." Then, putting her lips close to my ear, she whispered, "Is *he* your boyfriend?"

"*Tita!*"

She backed off and said, "I can't help it if I notice these things. So what's your mom doing in New York? Looking for a new husband?"

"She works for Flescher and Simmons. It's a graphics design company."

Caloy raised his head again. I wished he wouldn't listen so closely. I should have asked him to get me a drink.

"Really? I didn't think Ludy still had it in her."

"I don't know what you mean."

"Oh, you know, the ambitious career woman and all. But I guess that's what happens when your husband leaves you for a younger woman. Oh my, I hope I haven't said anything to upset you."

"It's too late now."

"I didn't know she was a citizen."

Always tell them I'm a green-card holder. That my company sponsored me. Then change the subject immediately. Never, ever tell them my real status.

"Her company sponsored her for a green card."

"Well, good for her. Does she have any plans to visit?"

"She ca—not yet. I don't think she's entitled to any vacations; she's very new at the job."

"I hope they haven't turned your mom into a slave."

"I'll send her your regards. She'll be happy to know that we met," I said, carefully untangling myself from her flabby arms.

"Thank God she's not a TNT," she said. "That would be just awful. That isn't what she is, Viola? Is she?" Honey's tongue was a carving knife, leaving deep impressions on my body. I would have gladly told her off, but instead I walked away, vowing never to be at the same party as she ever again.

Suddenly I felt Caloy next to me, guiding me toward the poolside. Neither of us said a word. I was afraid that if I opened my mouth, I would burst into tears. I could tell what he was thinking; I saw it in his eyes when he heard that my mother was living in New York. I'm sure he heard the part about TNT, too. Could he report her? I knew he was going to ask me about my mother. Let him.

"So she's a TNT? Big deal," I would say. *"She's not stealing. I could think of worse professions. She could even be a maid, heaven forbid. Someday, she'll get a green card. Someday she'll ask for me. Someday she'll come home.*

"You must miss your mother," he said as he helped me take a seat by the pool.

Because his voice was so earnest, I replied, "Big time."

I had nothing to hide.

Caloy left for the U.S. two days later. The wedding turned out to be a much bigger spectacle than anyone had anticipated. Not only did all fifteen hundred invited guests arrive, but an anti-Marcos rally went on just outside the Cathedral doors, its three hundred protesters shouting, "Cory! Cory! Cory!" Sylvia fainted from the heat just as the priest pronounced them "man and wife," and Doña Loleng got so drunk at the reception that she had to be sent home in a police-escorted limousine. The president showed up as expected, but he looked so ill that for once nobody wanted to come near him.

It was impossible for Caloy and me to find any time alone together. There were too many people vying for his company, and I wasn't about to make a beeline for his attention. Of course I was interested in him, but did it have to be obvious? On his last day in Manila, he surprised me by walking into the bookstore just before heading out to the airport.

I was in the middle of helping two high school students when I saw him stride through the glass doors, turning his head this way and that, trying to find me. In jeans and a T-shirt, he looked a lot younger than his twenty-five years. When he finally saw me, he rushed over and handed me a piece of paper. On it he had written his name (*Charlie* Austria), address, and phone number. He also gave me the number of the library. When he wasn't in his room, he said, that was the only other place he would be. As an afterthought, he wrote down the name of a friend, "in case of an emergency." He had written down a man's name, adding playfully, "I don't have any girlfriends."

"I'll keep in touch," he said, as he bent down to kiss me on the forehead. "See you at Christmas when I come back. Unless," he chuckled, "you miss me and decide to come and see me sooner."

The two of us ignored the students standing awkwardly beside us. I almost kissed him on the lips. When he left, I kept one hand next to me. The hand he had held. I didn't want anyone else to touch it.

18

The 1985 election came and went. Marcos won. Three months later, in February, our Saturday Circle meeting was canceled because there weren't enough members present. Those of us who did show up decided to go to the Manila Peninsula Hotel and hang out in the lobby. When we got there, there was an unusually loud buzz in the air. Jerome pulled one of the waiters aside and asked what the fuss was all about. We saw his eyes widen in direct proportion to the size of his open mouth.

He came back to us breathless and said that Defense Minister Juan Ponce Enrile and Armed Forces Vice Chief of Staff Fidel E. Ramos had just defected from the Marcos government and declared Corazon Aquino the duly elected president of the Philippines. The November election was a fraud. The two men were now at Enrile's headquarters in Camp Aguinaldo, calling for Marcos to resign. They were prepared to stay there and defend the country for as long as they could, even if it meant being finished off by Marcos in the process.

Balls. That's what Enrile and Ramos had. Hard, native balls. We knew they were pissed off at Marcos; that was what this was all about. Using the country simply made them look good to the public and foreign press. The two renegades, long cut off from Marcos's circle, were now indulging in a belated temper tantrum. Let them fight it out with the president. There was no need for the rest of the country to get involved.

But shortly after midnight, *yaya* came rushing into my bedroom to tell me that she had just heard Jaime Cardinal Sin over the radio, appealing to the Filipino people to go to EDSA and support Ramos and Enrile, to pray to Our Lady for peace. For the Cardinal to go on the air and make that announcement was like receiving a direct order from God Himself. The irony of the military and the civilians reversing their roles must be an act of God. Who was I to question or debate divine will?

For the next four days, EDSA became *the* party, the place to be and to be seen. I remember going to the Polo Club to watch my father in a tennis tournament, only to learn that the tournament had been canceled. There was hardly anyone around. I waited for my father, but he never showed up.

On the long and narrow stretch of highway, people from all points of Metro Manila, and perhaps other parts of the country as well, congregated to protect Enrile, Ramos, and their handful of followers from the pro-Marcos forces of the military.

I was there with Cecilia, Libeth, Jerome, *yaya,* and Eladio. We brought baskets of food, straw mats, folding chairs, and an ice chest filled with Coke. We had no idea how long we were going to be there. Before leaving for EDSA, Cecilia and I tried calling Connie's house to get her to join us, but no one answered the phones. Maybe they had all gone to the presidential palace.

We arrived there early Sunday morning, left our car on one of the side streets, and walked the rest of the way toward Camp Crame, where Enrile and Ramos had set up their joint headquarters. Every possible approach to the camp was barricaded with empty cars, buses lying on their sides, and burning rubber tires. I had never seen so many people in my life. Young, old, children, wealthy, poor, foreigners, priests, and nuns. Class and color disappeared in a single resolve to get rid of Marcos and stand in solidarity behind Enrile and Ramos.

After walking for more than an hour, we found a spot a few meters outside the camp and settled down with our mats and food. The others, who had arrived much earlier, were lying underneath open umbrellas, reading books or magazines, listening to the radio, or waking up from their naps to eat. A few enterprising men sold crackers and ice-cold water to passersby. Everyone else was deep in prayer, either by themselves or with others. The only occasion I could think of that came close to this was November 1, All Saints Day, when every Filipino flocked to the cemeteries and paid respect to their dead relatives.

At EDSA, everyone kept watch over Marcos's movements, wondering what would happen next. That afternoon the first army tanks appeared on Ortigas Avenue, less than a kilometer from the camp. I saw throngs of people rush toward them, hands outstretched, begging the tanks to stop, warning the soldiers of the blood that would blemish their hands for the rest of their lives. As if on cue, statues of the Virgin Mary and Jesus Christ on the Cross suddenly appeared. Murmurs of prayer ebbed and rose in waves. The soldiers, most of whom looked barely out of their teens, appeared confused and out of place. In their ill-fitting combat uniforms, they tried to look fierce and menacing, their machine guns slung across their chests, grenades quivering from their hip holsters. One soldier had his hand on a tear-gas canister, his fingers alternately tightening and loosening around it, ready to hurl it at a moment's command.

Then, out of the chorus rose a single voice reciting the "Hail

Mary." People knelt, mesmerized by the power of prayer, every hand clutching a rosary. A teenager appeared with a basket of fresh daisies and orchids, took a few awkward steps toward one tank, and held out a single daisy to the soldier closest to her. He neither flinched nor returned her gaze. Then a child followed, approaching another soldier, offering him a paper cutout of a heart. When the soldier didn't take it, the child boldly slipped it between his chest and his gun. A matron with a rosary and a cross in either hand walked from one soldier to another, stuffing their pockets with candy.

The soldiers remained unrelenting as drops of sweat trickled from beneath their helmets. An emboldened young man climbed up on the tank and offered a lit cigarette to a soldier. I saw the fear in the soldier's eyes. He was more afraid of this one cigarette than he was of the firepower he nervously cradled in his arms. He didn't move, but the young man coaxed and cajoled, refusing to give up. The soldier looked around at his comrades, his face begging for rescue. They simply looked back at him. The crowd began to shout, "Go on, take it!"

After a few more minutes, he broke down and took a puff. Everyone applauded and screamed, *"Mabuhay!"*, To life. Shortly after, the tanks backed off and moved somewhere else.

For the next few days, being at EDSA was like being at the world's largest family reunion. I saw people I hadn't seen in a long time and made new friends of strangers I might otherwise never have met. Filipinos who had been divided, conquered, and ruled by one man for twenty-one years couldn't hug and kiss each other enough. I bumped into my father and Carol, decked in head-to-foot campaign CORYphernalia: *yellow* espadrilles, *yellow* leggings, a *yellow* T-shirt emblazoned with Cory's face, a *yellow* straw hat with a Cory doll pinned on the brim, and a maid who followed her around holding a *yellow* umbrella over her head. As I passed my father, he mumbled in my ear, "She dragged me here."

On the third day, Cecilia and I decided to follow a group of soldiers who had defected to the Enrile-Ramos side, who were marching in single file toward the gates of Camp Crame. We had a wild idea of trying to find our way inside the campgrounds and all the way to Enrile and Ramos to ask for their autographs. But as we got closer to the gates, people began swarming around the soldiers, touching them, grabbing pieces of their uniform as if they were movie stars. It was too late for Cecilia and me to back out.

I grabbed at the back pocket of Cecilia's pants as she screamed, "Hang on! Hang on!" All I could see was the ponytail on her head. I felt myself being lifted and carried forward, took a deep breath, closed my eyes, and waited for this to end.

It was over in a second. Cecilia and I were inside, standing by ourselves between two rows of young civilians, who were now applauding us and acknowledging our presence with wolf whistles and howls. I looked at Cecilia, who was waving back at the men, blowing kisses with her hand. Without thinking, I raised my hand and waved too. For the first time in my life, I knew what it was like to be a beauty queen.

We never made it to Enrile and Ramos. Instead, we walked around the grounds, which were filled with the foreign press, socialites, the clergy, and military personnel guarding the idle Sikorsky helicopters. Ever since Corazon Aquino won the election, it had become fashionable to be anti-Marcos. People who were never pro or anti any political issue were suddenly taking stands. Or perhaps they were just opportunists, smart enough to recognize a trend and latch onto it.

The Crame grandstand had a streamer that read WELCOME DEFECTION CENTER. Cecilia and I tried to get in the line of a television camera, hoping that a journalist would interview us, but our tactics didn't work. We settled instead for a *Time* magazine photographer who asked us to pose next to a soldier, the three of us flashing the L-sign for *Laban*-fight—that was Cory's campaign slogan. "This better appear in the U.S. edition," I told the photographer. I wanted my mother and Caloy to see me.

Then, suddenly, He was there. Standing no more than ten feet away, dressed in a vest and army fatigues, the sleeves rolled up his elbow, the Philippine flag sewn upside-down on his left. On his body was slung a pair of Uzis, a black mobile phone, and the thickest mustache I ever saw. I walked closer to where he was being interviewed by several press people; he had to be a big shot, otherwise why would they bother with him? I couldn't hear what he was saying, only that he had a low, husky voice that didn't trip and stammer.

Our eyes met. He nodded politely toward me and smiled. Overwhelmed by all the prayer, love, and physical exhaustion that had been swirling around me during the past three days, I did what came naturally to me. I fainted. As I blissfully surrendered my body to the grass, my last conscious thought was how smart it was of me to have worn my new bikini underwear.

I don't know how long I was out, but when I came to, there was Cecilia frantically fanning me, and several faces I didn't recognize looking down at me. My soldier wasn't among them. I was lifted onto a stretcher and carried to an ambulance, where a nurse thrust an ammonia-soaked cotton ball at my nose. A doctor felt my pulse and forehead, asked how I was, and when I said I was fine, dismissed me promptly.

"Did you see him? Did you see him?" I asked Cecilia as we

walked toward the exit. She had no idea who I was talking about.

Just then I recognized one of the journalists who had interviewed my soldier. With a sudden burst of energy, I broke away
from Cecilia and rushed to the journalist.

"Excuse me, sir, but who was that soldier you were interviewing earlier?"

"Which one, sweetie?" he asked.

"The handsome one. He had a mustache."

"Oh him. That's Gringo Honasan, Enrile's chief security officer. Got the hots for him?"

Cecilia had caught up with me by then and abruptly pulled
me away. *Gringo, Gringo,* I said over and over, my heart getting
larger with every mention of his name.

On the fourth day of our vigil, there was another confrontation. Again a massive swell of people rose and rushed to the
tanks, pushing them back with their bare hands, armed only with
their rosaries and unwavering faith. This time, several gunships
circled above, the snarl of their engines a reminder that they
could blow us all apart. No one talked of leaving, no one talked
of fear. How could we be afraid when we had each other for
protection? When we had the power of divine protection? Guns
and bullets were nothing against the "Our Father" and "Let
There Be Peace on Earth."

The tanks could move no farther, their engines growling in
frustration at the stalemate between military might and prayer.
Uzi-carrying marines appeared out of the turrets and jumped
down to surround the tanks, their guns aimed at us. The chorus
of "Hail Marys" was much louder this time, reaching from one
end of EDSA to the other. Not even Rambo could have with-
stood it.

I eyeballed one Uzi and stared death in the face. I saw the
man I would never marry, the mother I would never become, the

child I would never hold, the life I would never live. I closed my eyes and fell on my knees, stretching out my arms, a rosary in either hand.

Then I heard guns being put away and footsteps receding. I opened my eyes and saw the soldiers preparing to leave. As I stood and watched them, I was suddenly compelled by a force rising within me. Without a second thought, I ran to a soldier and embraced him, Uzi and all, giving him a big kiss on the cheek. Other people followed, grabbing soldiers and holding them to their bosoms, one Filipino to another. The soldiers and tanks stopped, paralyzed by this massive swell of emotion. There was nothing else they could do.

That midnight, we learned that the Marcoses had fled.

When I returned home sometime after three in the morning, the maids said that Caloy and my mother had been calling, my mother in particular, frantically looking for me. Caloy had called to say how proud he was of me. My mother was a different story. She had been watching the news on television, and she was afraid I was in terrible danger. The maids had told her that I had hardly been home, that I was at EDSA most of the time. That's when my mother got hysterical, yelled, and told them to call the police. When I tried to call her back, all I got was an answering machine.

Shortly after, Ferdinand Marcos and his family and cronies fled the country, the Manila papers were filled with stories of how much the Marcoses had stolen and a list of what they had eaten for their last meal, as well as pictures of Imelda Marcos's shoe collection and Imelda and George Hamilton in various states of embrace. There were also conflicting reports about the exact number of people who were at EDSA. One paper said five hundred thousand, another estimated eight million, the entire population of Metro Manila.

The newspapers also published a list of individuals who were considered "the plunderers of the country's wealth." A travel ban was imposed on them, and their passports were invalidated pending the outcome of the new government's investigation.

I didn't know about the list until someone in school pointed it out to me. I immediately recognized several names that I had read about in the society pages. A few of them had even been guests at our house. There were also two I knew from direct association. One was Cosme Pilapil, Connie's father. The other was Diosdado Dacanay, my father.

He finally made it to *that* circle after all.

19

March 2

My dear Viola,

    My prayers have been answered! Thank God the Marcoses are out and you're safe back home again. But Viola, what were you thinking, endangering your life like that at EDSA? Did you think you were going to be a hero? They don't make heroes anymore. Next time, just watch it on TV!

Love, Mom

Watch the People Power Revolution on TV? I can't believe she said that, after all that had happened. The latest news report on my father mentioned the possibility of sequestering Galaxy Books and Publishing and auctioning off its assets. Another possibility was the appointment of a caretaker administration until Daddy and the business received a clean bill of health. No one really knew for sure how quickly this would happen or get resolved, although the list of "plunderers" had now increased from the original twenty to forty-three.

Dad took this all in stride. I suspect he was secretly thrilled to be on the list because it meant that he was in the same company as the big-name people mentioned there. The first time I saw that list two weeks ago, I didn't know what to do. That's probably why Connie hadn't shown up at school. When I called her at home, the maids said that she wasn't around.

I immediately called Daddy at work, but his secretary told me he hadn't arrived. She hadn't read the papers that morning and hadn't heard anything unusual. "Why, Miss Viola, have the Marcoses returned?" I tried reaching Daddy in Dasmariñas, but he wasn't there either. He hadn't come home the night before, and Carol and Jake had just left that morning for Nueva Vizcaya, where she's from.

My first thought was that Daddy had slipped out of the country and left me holding the bag. I could see myself standing before the PCGG, the Philippine Commission on Good Government, explaining my parents' whereabouts. When Connie finally showed up in school, she told Cecilia and me that her parents had left for Lisbon on the last night of the revolution. Apparently they'd always had an apartment there for something like this. Poor Connie, she'd aged so much she looked as if she was in her thirties. She had been left behind to look after Doña Loleng, who was too old to travel and had been in and out of the hospital. Connie said that all her *lola* talked about was Bobadilla.

The worst part about Dad's absence was that I couldn't call the police. So when he finally showed up in our house two days later, I was relieved. But he looked awful. He said he had been with his lawyer for the past thirty-six hours, discussing the investigation and his and the bookstore's liabilities. His lawyer assured him that the real target of the investigation was Tee Pak Long and the money he had lent to Daddy to expand the bookstore. Apparently Long was Marcos's top gold courier from way back. The PCGG was eager to determine if Dad knowingly used the money in spite of Long's reputation, and if the bookstore was in fact a dummy corporation for Marcos. Unfortunately, Long was in one of the helicopters that flew the Marcoses out of Malacañang Palace. It was assumed that he was now hiding somewhere in Switzerland.

Daddy told me not to worry. His lawyer said that, as far as the government was concerned, Dad was small fry. My father looked insulted when he told me this, which was probably why, more than the investigation itself, he looked the way he did. "All we can do right now is wait and see and look as if nothing's happened," he said. "Just be careful about what you say and who you speak to. You never know who's listening, or whose side people are on nowadays."

That was a mere two weeks ago. Nowadays, Dad appears to have recovered fully and is back to his old self. Carol has begun showing her face at the Polo Club again. Last weekend, he threw a belated anniversary party at the Manila Peninsula to celebrate the founding of Galaxy Books and Publishing. He said that he also wanted to use the opportunity to welcome me officially into the company as a member of the next generation of management. I wish Dad would reserve his lies for Carol and his girlfriends.

To his credit, the party was quite *the* bash and dispelled any rumors that he was in big trouble. He even had Senator Bimbo Magsanoc as a special guest of honor. Magsanoc just happens to sit on the PCGG's advisory board and is also a frequent tennis partner of Peping Cojuangco, Cory's brother. I wouldn't be surprised if Dad tells me next that he's having lunch with Cory.

I never got introduced at the party as Daddy had said I would. Instead he announced that he was going to be a father for the third time. He was so drunk by ten o'clock that he threw up on the dance floor and collapsed on one of the hotel's sofas.

At the same party, I got to meet Dad's lawyer, who was surprised that "Dado had such a sophisticated daughter." The lawyer wanted to know how to get in touch with my mother and whether she was ever aware of Tee Pak Long's activities. He thought that might help establish Daddy's innocence. "In case we need your mom to testify on your father's behalf," he said. "Why would she want to do that?" I asked. "Because anything that happens to Galaxy Books will affect your mother. She stands to lose just as much," he said.

March 21

Viola,

WHO is Charlie Austria? I thought you said it was Caloy. Are they one and the same person? The other day, I returned from my lunch break and there were all these message slips from him. Of course Cassandra, she's the office receptionist who thinks of herself as a fashion plate, thinks that I have a boyfriend. I didn't bother to dispute what she thought. How did he get my number? Didn't I tell you not to give it to anyone? What does he do? Where does he live? Who are his parents? What do they do? Where do they live? Viola, I hope this isn't anything serious. Take care.

Your mom

March 25

Dear Viola,

Well, well, guess who I spoke to today? My God, why didn't you tell me that Caloy Austria was THE Austria of

Austria Lumber? Your father and I used to bump into his parents at parties. It's a shame they never made it to any of ours, although I never stopped trying. Kikay Austria's diamonds were just to DIE for! Of course, I always pretended that her diamonds didn't impress me. I can be very subtle when it comes to things like that.

I was on the phone when Cassandra handed me a slip that a Charlie Austria was on the other line. She hung around my desk pretending that she was looking for something, when in fact she was trying to eavesdrop. I got rid of her by saying that it was already 4:45, which is the time she always leaves the office. Anyway, when I picked up my phone, I was very impressed by the way Caloy introduced himself. "Please forgive me for being forward. My name is Charlie Austria, and I met Viola at the wedding of Sylvia Pilapil. My parents are Ruperto and Kikay Austria. I think they know you because I've heard my mother speak of you a number of times." Now tell me, wasn't that very nice? He even asked me how I preferred to be called: Mrs. Dacanay or Ms. Sanvictores. Of course I told him to drop the formalities and just call me tita Ludy.

He called to invite me to join his family for Easter Sunday, but I said that I already had a previous commitment. He said that it would be just him, his brother Totoy, who is a junior at Columbia, and his sister Irene and her American husband, Mark. They live in Princeton and have a four-year-old named Savanna Marie Austria O'Shea. He said that his parents were making their annual trip to the Vatican. His mother cannot stand New York at this time of year because of her severe seasonal allergies.

I told him that we would just have to set another day when he's in town. He tries to come every two months to see his family. He also told me that he has just one more year to go before he finishes with his MBA. Before we hung up, he gave me his number at the dorm, the library (the only other place he could be found) and his friend's (you'll be relieved to know it was a man) for emergency. He also gave me the address and phone number of their place in Manhattan, in case I ever needed anything. Totoy (whose real name is Albert) lives there full-time, he said. He did warn me about his brother, though. It turns out that Totoy cannot make up his mind about a major and has shifted for the third time. He's now a Greek classics major.

Wow! Viola, what did you do to this man? He even told me that he hasn't had a serious relationship in a long time. I thought that was a curious thing to tell me.

This is all for now. Let's see what happens next. Take care.

Kisses, Mommy

April 1

Dear Viola,

I just thought I'd send you a Xerox copy of the Easter card Caloy sent me. It came with a huge floral arrangement of Easter lilies and purple hydrangeas. Anything new with your father and the PCGG? Why haven't they arrested him yet? The only problem there is that there isn't a prison large enough to hold his ego.

Mom

April 5

Viola,

I can't believe I've been living here for two years! As you can imagine, work has settled into a predictable and comfortable routine. In the beginning, it felt as if my life was on an express train, and the only things I saw outside were image distortions and flashpoints of light. But now I'm okay. My boss is a woman named Heather. She repeats every sentence twice and carefully enunciates her syllables. I used to think she did this for my benefit, but she's that way with everyone. She's probably not yet in her thirties, but the feathery lines around her eyes give her more years than she probably deserves.

When I was first hired, my tasks were pretty much limited to filing, answering phones, confirming appointments. Menial stuff. Lately, I've been handling most of Heather's business correspondence and now and then I deal with clients when she isn't around. It makes me feel like a hostess for a big party but, of course, I know my place. I think about my life in Manila and my life here, and how much of it has changed. I think the biggest change for me was coming to terms with the fact that I am no longer a socialite. A woman who used to have servants, a driver, social status, wealth, a family. I guess it shouldn't bother me that much. It's not like losing one's face. As a TNT, I no longer have any face to speak of.

Mom

April 8

Vi,

It's not easy being a TNT. Every day I am reminded that my life can detonate at the mere mention of that other three-letter word, the INS. I think of it as a big, fat cat hiding in a dark, secluded alley, ready to pounce on my hopes and dreams. The first lie is always the toughest. All others simply get easier. Over time, I've learned to go from one lie to the other, making up elaborate tales, creating fictional lives, always hoping that no one is keeping track of my stories. Just for your info, my official bio goes something like this: I was born in Hawaii. My father was a pineapple picker in Maui. He took the family back to the Philippines when I was around four. That takes care of any questions people may ask about my citizenship and lack of an American accent. I also tell them that I was in the clothing business before I came over.

Sometimes my lies catch up with me, but I recover quickly. Even my names have become parts of my disguise. To my bank, I am Lourdes Sanvictores Dacanay; in the office I am known as Lou Sanvictores; and then, of course, there's Ludy Dacanay. It's odd thinking in the third person. Three versions of one person, three different lives. So much more than the life I had in Manila: stuck with one life forever.

I cannot afford to get caught. But fear is an illusion conjured by a mind that lacks control. The trick is to condition the mind and turn fear into an ally. But most of all, the bottom line is coming to terms with the solitary existence of a TNT. Never seen or heard, talking about ourselves in whispers. Invisible people. Of course there are others like me, escaping old lives and beginning new ones. Each of us with this BIG secret. Despite our common experience, we are alienated from each other precisely because of it.

You never know who is a TNT. Even the next person could be one. It's not like there are support groups for TNTs. Wouldn't a TNT Anonymous sound funny? Knowing there are

others like me doesn't ease the loneliness. So why am I a TNT?
Because right now, it's the only way I know to stay alive.

Mom

It doesn't bother her that she's a TNT. That she lies. She said I'm the only person she's told. Of course I would never do anything to hurt her. Does that make me a liar too?

Memorandum

TO: Diosdado Dacanay
Chairman and CEO
Galaxy Books and Publishing

FROM: Members of the Board*
Galaxy Books and Publishing

DATE: May 16, 1986

RE: SUSPENSION by a Board Resolution

Pending the outcome of the Philippine Commission on Good Government's investigation into the activities of Mr. Tee Pak Long and his EXACT association with Galaxy Books and Publishing, the board of directors, by unanimous vote, has decided, in the best interest of said company, to suspend **without pay** Diosdado Dacanay from his present duties as Chairman and CEO.

That in doing so, the Board recognizes that Mr. Dacanay is not absolved and/or exempted from past and current liabilities with regard to said company.

That the Board will act in Mr. Dacanay's capacity until the investigation is resolved.

That the Board will ensure his presence and co-operation as well as that of the bookstore when the PCGG sends in its team of auditors acting under the supervision of the Bureau of Internal Revenue on May 31.

That the Board will not shoulder Mr. Dacanay's legal expenses, although, should the need arise, it will extend financial assistance as the Board deems appropriate.

Should Mr. Dacanay wish to appeal this resolution, he has thirty days to respond. In the meantime, he is free to appoint a representative on his behalf, provided that said representative is duly approved by the Board.

THIS MEMORANDUM TAKES EFFECT IMMEDI-ATELY UPON ITS RECEIPT.

*Signed: Paquito Quiros
            Emmanuel Arroyo
            Florentino Colayco
            Aloysius Goduco
            Raul Pagaspas
            Hector Silos

cc: Philippine Commission on Good Government *FOR INTER-NAL DISTRIBUTION ONLY*

May 26

Viola!

Who are the members of the PCGG? What happened to your father's friend, that Senator Bimbo something? You better not let anyone near our house. DON'T let them take my mango tree away!

Mom

20

July 11

My dear Viola,

*I had the oddest experience just yesterday. I happened to be
in Manhattan for a couple of hours and decided to call your
mom at work to see if she was available to join me for lunch.
When I called Flescher and Simmons, a receptionist told me that
your mom had quit her job and left for Manila because her
mother had died. At first I thought I got my dates or numbers
wrong because your mom had called me the night before, although she didn't leave any message. Didn't you tell me that
both sets of your grandparents were already dead? I hope she
tries and calls again.*

Yours always, Caloy

I read Caloy's letter again and again, trying to make sense
of his words. The date on his letter said the 11th, five days
ago. My mother's last letter to me was dated sometime the end
of June. I had not heard from her since. That didn't surprise me.
In her book of accounting, I owed her a letter. But Caloy's letter

sounded urgent; he seemed worried. At first I thought she was hiding from him—in her usual way, she didn't want to seem eager for his friendship or appear that she was encouraging a relationship between him and me. Even though I knew—and *she* knew—that that was what she had in mind.

I let a few days pass before I called Flescher and Simmons myself. It was Cassandra on the other line. I proceeded cautiously, I didn't give her my name.

"May I speak to Lou Sanvictores, please?" I said.

"Is this personal or business?" she asked.

"Personal. We were supposed to meet after work today," I replied.

Cassandra said, "She no longer works here." I felt my stomach drop to the floor. "Must be in the Philippines by now," she added. "Try her in Manila if you know where to reach her. And *who* is this again?"

I hung up quickly.

I called my mother's apartment next. A recorded voice said that the number *is not in service for incoming calls.* My mother couldn't be dead; I would have heard from the Philippine Consulate, from her friends, and even from my father.

When my parents were still together, it was not unusual for my mother to disappear when my father's womanizing *really* got on her nerves. She would go off by herself and spend a couple of days, sometimes a week, with a close friend in another city, until her anger subsided. Or until Dad or I, or the two of us together, brought her home. She was never incommunicado, nor did she go too far away. She always left an address or number lying around in a place where she knew someone would "accidentally" find it.

Once, however, she decided to take me—without my asking—on one of her disappearing acts. It happened right after their tenth wedding anniversary when Dad had presented Mom with a fabulous South Sea pearl choker.

That night, we were having dinner at the L'Hirondelle. The waiter had just filled our crystal flutes with more champagne when my father took out a light gray velvet box from his coat pocket and placed it before my mother.

My mother sat there impassively, her face unimpressed, her arms tightly crossed against her chest. In his seat, my father looked like a little boy waiting for a pat on the head. I was eager to see what he was giving her and mildly irritated at her for keeping me in suspense.

You don't have to forgive him, Ma. Just take the damn thing!

"May I?" I said finally, to break the silence, and reached out for the box. My mother remained tight-lipped. My father looked totally silly. As I flipped the lid wide open, I was struck, not by the luminescent spheres, but by a white linen card resting against the gold-and-diamond hibiscus clasp. Written on the card, in beautiful calligraphy, was another woman's name.

My mother had seen the name too, and before I could take the card away, she grabbed the box from my hands and yanked it out. She looked at the card and then at my father. Her *uh-oh* was neither angry nor sarcastic. It sounded as if she had just noticed a run in her pantyhose.

My father jerked as the cold bubbly spilled onto his pants; his knee hit the table with a loud thud. While he grimaced and squirmed, an alert waiter came over with a napkin, poised to pat him dry. But my father shooed the young man away. My mother watched him with icy detachment. Then, for the first time since we arrived at the restaurant, she actually smiled. She pushed her hands against the table, grabbed her evening purse, and stood up.

Leaning toward my father, she whispered in his dazed face, "Next time, at least try to get one of us right!"

She turned around and walked away. I made a move to follow her, then I stopped and walked back to my father. He just sat there, staring at the necklace. Placing my hand on his arm, I said to him, "I'm sorry I wasn't fast enough." He looked up at me, patted my hand, and nodded gently. "It's all right. Just go with your mother," he said. By the time I caught up with her, she was sitting inside a cab, waiting for me. My father didn't come home until the next morning.

On hindsight, I realize I should have taken the necklace. I would never be able to afford something like that in my lifetime. My father had really outdone himself. It's a shame I never saw the necklace again. My father knew better than to give her something else in exchange.

Two days later, my mother and I were at the Mandarin Hotel, registering under the names of our maids. The only thing she said to me before we left our house was, "Pack a bag. Bring a couple of school uniforms."

As soon as we walked into our hotel suite, I began to feel claustrophobic. I was not impressed by the damask draperies. The huge fresh-fruit basket looked fake to me; the chandelier and mahogany furniture were funereal. I wasn't going to sleep here.

"What if Daddy doesn't find us?" I asked my mother. She said nothing. What if my father took her seriously, just to teach her a lesson? What if I never saw my house and my room again? I picked up the phone and dialed my father's direct line at the office. He was surprised; he didn't even know we were missing.

My father knocked on our door an hour later, and my mother meekly followed him home. She never took me on an excursion again.

Now I called my father at home to see if he had heard any news about my mother. I was careful to keep the alarm out of my voice. He was surprised by my call and happy to chat with me. From his voice I could tell that he had no clue about my mother's whereabouts, so I said I had to run.

I was up the whole night with a migraine. A list of shoulds kept running in my head: I *should* have written that letter. I *should* have called. It occurred to me that I didn't know if my mother had other friends. I *should* have gone with my mother. Now it was too late. Perhaps I should call Caloy and ask him to look for my mother. Shit! What will Caloy think of me? Of my family? He'll think we're a bunch of low-class losers.

Unless my mother was on her way home and wanted to surprise me. But it doesn't take that long to fly from New York to Manila. Unless she stopped in California or Hawaii first. It was easier to deal with fantasy than with either of my parents. I said a prayer to St. Jude, asking for a sign that my mother was okay. Asking for a sign that she would come back to me.

Two days later, I received a letter from my mother.

My dearest Viola,

The past week and a half have been absolutely crazy for me and it is only now that things are getting back to normal and I can finally write to you.

Last July 7, Dede called me at work, on the verge of a nervous breakdown. It turned out that the friend through whom she, I, and several others had acquired our fake Social Security cards had been caught in a sting operation by INS and FBI agents. The friend, who was now identified as Philip Malixi, a Filipino-American living in Hoboken, had been on their wanted list for a long time, but they never had enough proof against him. Dede suspected that someone—probably a rival in the same business—had squealed on this person. "The guy's been around

*for so long, why only now?" she said. What threw us all into
a fit was that Malixi, in exchange for a lighter sentence, agreed
to turn over his diary containing the names of his clients. THE
JERK!! We had no idea if we were on that list.*

*As soon as I got off the phone, I went to the ladies' room
and locked myself inside one of the cubicles. My God, Viola, I
kept praying, "Why now? Just when things were going so well
for me. Oh Lord, not now!" What if my name was in that diary? Can you imagine the horror of having the FBI and the
INS coming into the office and handcuffing me? And the press!
I don't want my face splattered all over* The New York
Times!

*I bit into my knuckles until my skin hurt. I was so afraid
I'd scream and give myself away. Then I heard Heather knocking
on the door, asking if everything was okay. I tried to shake her
off by saying I was fine, but she didn't want to leave me alone.
So I had no choice but to come out and talk to her.*

*"Oh my! What's happened?" she asked. Before I could stop
myself, I leaned over her shoulder and began to cry. It must
have been her face that did it for me. Or maybe her Dior perfume
that I remembered so well on my own mother.*

*"I just got a call from the Philippines," I told her. "My
mother died a few hours ago."*

*Thank God I'm a quick thinker. I made up some story
about how "my mother" had been ill for some time with lung
cancer and how the doctors in Manila had assured me that at
her age, the cancer would take longer to spread. I felt so guilty
afterward because when I looked up at Heather, I saw that she
was crying too.*

*She asked me when I was going home. What a perfect
excuse! I'm glad she thought of it. She offered to arrange my*

leave of absence with personnel. When I returned to my desk, several of the staff members were already there, waiting to express their condolences. Our personnel manager told me to take the rest of the day off. After everyone had gone back to their desks, I discreetly emptied mine of all my personal belongings. I had made up my mind that I was not going to return ever again.

That afternoon, I mailed Flescher and Simmons my letter of resignation, packed a few things, and went directly to Dede's place. I canceled my phone and had my mail held at the post office. Had you written to me, I would have gotten your letter just the same.

For several days, Dede and I stayed indoors. We didn't answer the phone, and we went out of the apartment only to attend mass.

We just sat, ate Spam, fried rice, and potato chips, read the newspapers, watched the news, and waited. We kept the TV on the whole time; we didn't want to block out the world completely. The odd thing was that the incident was mentioned only once on network TV, and it wasn't even in The New York Times. *It received more coverage in the Filipino papers, but not for long. It turned out that Malixi's diary didn't have the kind of list the FBI wanted after all, and now his lawyer was suing the INS for wrongful arrest.*

After ten days, I felt it was safe to go back to my apartment. Dede thought about moving to the Midwest, but I told her that they ate only corn and potatoes out there. Dede couldn't live without rice.

When I returned to my building, my super greeted me warmly. Before leaving I had told him that I was going away, but I didn't tell him where. He said he was glad to see me back. I quickly nodded my thanks and headed straight for my apartment. I had just gotten to my floor when he yelled that in my

*absence I had received some flowers. He said that he had saved
the cards and slipped them under my door.*

*They were condolence cards from the staff of Flescher and
Simmons, and from Caloy. He must have called the office. How
embarrassing!*

*I don't know what I'm going to do next. I still have to
worry about this Immigration Reform and Control Act (IRCA)
that the U.S. Congress is about to pass. It's supposed to penalize
employers who knowingly hire illegal aliens, and at the same
time grant amnesty to those who arrived in America during a
certain period. Unfortunately, my arrival date is not covered by
that program. Isn't life funny? If it isn't one thing, it's another.
I know God has a sense of humor: I just don't understand why
I always seem to be the punchline of his jokes.*

*In any case, don't worry about me. Despite everything else,
I REALLY AM FINE! I have enclosed my new phone number
and also that of your* tita *Dede's. By the way, in case Caloy
calls or writes to you, DON'T say a word about any of this.
Just before my "disappearing act," I had called him but just left
my name on his machine. I just hope that he didn't speak to
Cassandra. Is there a way for you to find out, do you think?*

This is all for now. Take care and write to me. I miss you.

Love, Mom

I said a prayer of thanks to St. Jude, but I worried about her
job prospects. I didn't even know if she still had enough money.
I hoped she wouldn't end up working as a domestic helper. My
God! I would personally drag her home.

21

Ever since my mother left for America and I began living by myself, my father has rarely set foot in what used to be our family home. Not that I kept him away, not that he needed an invitation. The only reason I could think of for his self-imposed distance was an inability to confront his past. I was therefore surprised when my father dropped by unannounced. I had just gotten off the phone with Caloy when I heard the doorbell ring. It was two in the morning and the maids were all in bed. I was not expecting anyone. When I looked out the window, I saw my father's car parked in front of the house. I ran to the gate to let him in. Outside, he was leaning against his car, alone. His appearance was disheveled. He had lost a lot of weight, and there were bald patches all over his head. He was wearing dark, almost black, glasses.

"What's happened to you?" I asked.

He brushed past me and headed for the den, where he slumped on the sofa. I left him to get a glass of water, bumping into *yaya,* who was standing in the hallway, ready to swing an ax. We both jumped backward in surprise. She thought there was an intruder. I told her it was only my father. She scowled and shoved the ax at me instead. *Yaya* has never forgiven him for leaving my mother and me. I told her to go back to bed, put the ax away, got the water, and returned to my father.

He was sitting now. Still avoiding any direct eye contact, he took the glass, set it on the coffee table, and stared at the ice cubes as they slowly melted. From where I sat I could feel him smoldering inside. The next thing I knew there was a fierce, hacking sound cutting through the den walls. It was my father, crying. I was beginning to resent the role of adult that my parents had placed on me. I wasn't even twenty!

"They're trying to destroy me! They're trying to destroy me!" he wailed.

"Who's they?"

"The PCGG. The BIR. They all want to take over Galaxy Books for themselves. They're using Tee Pak Long so that no one will accuse them of being thieves. They're all the same! They just got rid of Marcos to make room for themselves and make up for lost time. This new government can't fool me. Marcos's hidden wealth? The country will never see that money ever again!"

I tried to calm my father down—but he was out of control. "They've threatened to take the Dasmariñas house away. They're putting pressure on the board to get rid of me. They've gotten to Carol. The bitch! She and the kids have left. She won't even let them see me."

When he looked up at me, I was shocked by the dark rings under his eyes. He had never looked so old and decrepit, so alone. His anguish played back for me all the years of my mother's pain: the elbow nudges and back-talk she endured, the women who confronted her and boasted that they were my father's girlfriends, the excuses she was always ready to recite on his behalf.

I remembered parties where the women had the nerve to sit

next to my mother, each of them looking like anxious beauty contestants, waiting for my father to crown them with his favor. But my father always outsmarted them. He stayed away, standing smugly at the bar the whole evening, drinking round after round of Chivas Regal and enjoying the envious nudges of his friends. He stayed away even from my mother. I never left her side. I always sat next to her, protecting her, making sure that she was never smeared with their filth.

I remembered those women now as I looked at my father, slouched against the sofa. I felt no compassion for him. He had lost whatever claim he may have had on my sympathy when he walked out on my mother. The man sitting before me just happened to be my progenitor.

"Why don't you stay for the night? You look as if you haven't slept for months," I offered.

I slowly tiptoed to the door, but as soon as I put my hand on the doorknob, he gave out a loud yawn and mumbled, "I just spoke to your mother."

I turned around in surprise. "When?"

"Yesterday, the day before—I don't remember."

"How did you know where to reach her?"

"Actually, she called me."

"What did she want from *you*?"

"She read the news about the BIR. She wanted to know where I was going to get the money to pay. She warned me not to involve this house, or we'd see each other in court." He rubbed the stubble on his chin, looking dazed. "Your mom's gotten pretty feisty, hasn't she? She didn't even ask how I was."

"After all that's happened, you actually expected her to?"

"Your mother and I agreed that, at least for now, it was best for you to join her in New York as soon as possible. She said she'll take care of everything."

My mother asked for me. She finally asked for me.

"What about school?"

"I don't expect this to last forever. What's a semester or two? For all you know, you could be back by Christmas. I've made arrangements with the American Embassy for your visa. Don't worry about your expenses. I'll send you money. Why don't you take a management seminar or something? Cooking class if you have to."

"Where will I stay?"

"With your mother, naturally."

"I wish she had called me herself."

"What difference does it make? You're going to see her. I'm tired now," he yawned. "If you don't mind, I'm going to sleep right here."

He put his legs on the sofa, kicked off his shoes, and rested his head on one of the pillows. Just before I left, I asked, "Was there any truth to Galaxy Books and Marcos?"

"No," he sighed. "Otherwise, we'd have a town house on Fifth Avenue by now." He closed his eyes and began to snore.

That night I couldn't sleep. I didn't like the idea of being tossed like a tennis ball between my parents until one or both of them got tired of the game. I was no longer sure I wanted to go. I was suddenly afraid to be with my mother. Had it really been two years since I last saw her?

I remembered the days leading up to her departure; they were like the aftermath of a natural disaster. *Get rid of your father's trophies, burn his clothes, send all your bills to your father, buy me a year's worth of Medicol aspirin, donate my wedding dress to the Hospicio de San José, don't forget to have masses said on the death anniversaries of my parents, don't ever let your father's mistress come anywhere within one kilometer of this house, count the silverware periodically, look after the mango tree.*

And as if our lives weren't dizzy enough, at the last minute I had decided that I *did* want to join her after all. I didn't want to be left in the house, or in Manila by myself. *I don't know what got into me in Rustan's*, I desperately explained to her. I still remember the look on her face, the flitting smile of accommodation, suddenly replaced by a look of such horrendous fear that I was sorry I had ever reversed myself.

She said that it was too late to apply for a U.S. visa; I should have changed my mind much earlier. She tried all sorts of tactics to get me to stay. She said something about the prom, something about her not having a job and having no immediate means of supporting herself, much less the two of us. But I was strong and forceful. I told her I could find a job. I reminded her about the fun, the adventure she and I would have living it up in New York. She only got more irritated. I knew it had nothing to do with me. She would have stayed rather than take me into the unknown with her.

"I don't want you with me."

When she said those words, it felt as if someone had just wrenched my heart out. I was surprised by how calmly I accepted what she had just said, as if she had told me that I needed a new haircut. For the first few weeks after she left, she'd call on the phone and end up speaking to the maids. I meant for it to be that way; I wasn't ready for a relationship with her, especially a long-distance one. I never told her that I was actually listening in on the extension, her voice so clear and so close I could almost feel her breath on my cheek. Letters were a lot easier to handle. She could say whatever she needed to say on those pretty note-cards of hers. I, on the other hand, could always throw them away when her absence threatened to overwhelm me. Which was often.

My mind was in a state of unrest, thinking and imagining all the things I would say to her when we met. I had rarely thought about our reunion. When she left, I had made a promise that I would see her only when she asked for me. And now she had, if somewhat indirectly. Did that count?

Would she be any different from the last time we were to-gether? What about me? After being apart, I was finally going to see what she looked like. Felt like. Know her in a way that I had not been able to the whole time she had been away. I was going to determine for myself, once and for all, whether her departure had *really* been worthwhile.

When I woke up the next day, my father was gone. His head hadn't even left a mark on the pillow.

22

There was no time to say good-bye, to be the honoree at any farewell party. My father felt that it was best for me to leave as quickly and quietly as possible. I was not to tell anyone that I was leaving, not even Cecilia. "You can always send her a postcard once you're there," he said.

The plane trip was long and uneventful. The Dramamine I had taken before boarding hadn't helped at all. I stayed awake through two movies, three meals, and numerous snacks. I must have put on five pounds in those fifteen hours alone. Conversations were of no use. At this altitude, they were as thin as air. The woman sitting next to me was pleasant enough until I realized she was trying to convert me. She mentioned something about being a Jehovah's Witness. Or was it a born-again Christian?

In the end, I found myself staring out the window, watching the sunrise through the purple haze of the horizon. It seemed days before I heard, "Flight attendants, prepare for landing."

After the touchdown, I decided to remain seated and calm my nerves. Across from the tarmac, I saw a field of tall grass, dried and yellowed from the sun. Behind it were uneven rows of faded buildings. I couldn't see the Empire State Building. Where was the Statue of Liberty?

Despite the flight attendant's urgent calls for everyone to remain seated, passengers elbowed their way toward the exit, clogging the aisles with their belongings. When the door finally swung open, I clutched the rosary inside my pocket and joined the long queue going out.

I hurriedly walked through the passageway, its gray walls filled with posters of New York City. At the arrival hall, I was surprised by the number of people standing there, cordoned off by red velvet ropes that snaked across the entire length of the room. A flight from London had apparently arrived a few minutes before ours.

"Get in line!" barked a young woman in a navy blue jacket, gray pants, white blouse, and a striped red-white-and-blue necktie. She walked up and down the lines saying, "Please have your passports ready." At the other end of the hall a man dressed in the same uniform was pointing imperiously at each arrival, "You, over to Window Seventeen! You, to your left at Window Five!"

The crowd bothered me. I had hoped to be out of the airport in the shortest possible time. I got in line behind a group of Japanese tourists who had Nikons and Sony Handycams dangling down their necks. One was already busy recording the scene, providing a running commentary in Japanese. Suddenly, a pair of six-footers with crew cuts jumped behind me, their hand-tooled leather valises throwing me off balance.

There was nothing to see or do other than move forward. Or listen to the airport security people bellow at us as, "THERE - IS - NO-EATING-NO-DRINKING-AND-NO-PICTURE-TAKING-ALLOWED - IN - THIS - ROOM - JUST - KEEP - THE - LINES - MOVING - FOLKS - AND - ONCE - AGAIN—"

I looked at the immigration officers sitting behind the glass partitions, perched on their stools like bank tellers. I tried to recall my mother's warning the last time we spoke on the phone, shortly before I left. I watched out for the booths that emptied out quickly, paid particular attention to the people who humbly submitted folder after folder for inspection.

I couldn't help but feel sorry for the Asian gentleman at Window 8 as the officer asked him, his irritation audible to the rest of us, "Once-again-how-long-are-you-staying-in-the-United-States?" And when it was clear that the man didn't speak English, the officer asked in exasperation if anyone in the room spoke "Chinese or wherever this person is from?"

Thirty minutes later, I was still no closer to the yellow line. My stomach was beginning to rumble. The number of people swelled as more flights arrived. The room became warm and stuffy. Additional uniformed personnel were fielded onto the floor to control the crowd, now showing signs of becoming testy and unruly.

This was not my idea of a welcome, to be inside a plane for fifteen hours and then be expected to stand around while everyone else went about their business, slapping each other on the backs as if the rest of us were not there. If *they* had traveled across time zones and continents as some of us had just done, they might have looked at our ordeal with a little bit more compassion.

Or maybe not.

As I looked around it was clear that a piece of the world had descended upon JFK Airport, each individual a tiny patch that belonged to a much larger canvas made up of shapes, colors, and sounds. Was this how the immigration officers perceived us? Or did they see us with their invisible laser eyes, scanning the deepest, darkest depths of our marrows, hoping to find the reasons for our coming to America? Deciding whether those reasons were good or not. Whether we were good enough.

What lives did each of us leave behind to get here? Who were we in real life? *Who am I?*

A group of Asian refugees in single file was escorted to a separate booth by a man who kept shouting, "Excuse me, passing through. Out! Out!"

Each of the refugees clutched a white plastic bag that contained the promise of a better life. They walked past us with heads bent, as if they were afraid someone might snatch the promise away from them. Or self-conscious because they had something that everyone else coveted.

"You!" the uniformed woman finally called out to me, "Step up to Window Eight, please!"

I walked carefully toward the cubicle, my mind and body filled with a bursting sense of awe and trepidation. I saw the Asian Oppressor watching my movements, his eyes never leaving my face, his radar scanning my soul. I gave my beads a final squeeze and walked brightly to the window.

"Good afternoon!"

Don't look overly confident. My mother said to me.

The bully didn't even bother to smile, just threw his open palm before me, flipped through my passport, looked at me, then down at my documents again.

Something snapped inside of me. *I was not my mother!* Her fears didn't have to be mine. I stopped sweating. This was going to be a piece of cake. My ordeal was over. The rest proceeded without further incident.

I had declined my mother's offer to meet me at the airport and hadn't even told her the date and time of my arrival. All she knew was that I would arrive on a Wednesday in August. I wasn't trying to be coy. I needed time to warm up to the idea of having a mother around again. She wasn't pleased with the secrecy, but she couldn't change it. I left a message on her answering machine to say that I was on my way, using the code she had given me. *"Dumapo na ang paru-paro."* The butterfly has landed. The words sounded like the dialogue from an awful Tagalog movie. I felt stupid saying them and put my mouth close to the phone, making sure that no one else heard me. I hopped into a Yellow cab waiting on line. It was 5:30 in the afternoon.

My driver was a Sikh Indian. In my best authoritative voice I gave him my mother's address and her specific instructions on how to get there. "They're going to try and take you the long way because they know you're new to the city. Be alert! Then they'll realize they're not dealing with some gullible tourist," she had said.

As the cab drove along Grand Central Parkway, I found myself unable to focus on the scenery flying before me. Cars and vans zipped past us, zigzagging across the lanes, shattering our eardrums with their horns.

"Oh, fuck you!" my Indian cowboy yelled, flipping an indignant middle finger at a blue Mustang that came unnecessarily close. He tilted his head in my direction and smiled an apology. "Sorry, miss."

I said nothing, just looked out the window. It occurred to me that that was all I'd been doing. From the corner of my eye, I saw him lift his chin to look at me through his rearview mirror. I felt the imminent beginnings of a conversation.

"First time to New York?"

I nodded curtly.

"Filipino?"

"Yes."

He let out a small scream of joy. "You see, you see, I get it right all the time. I should have made a bet with you. I'm an expert at telling faces; Swedes, Norwegians, Japanese, Thais, I can guess them all. It also helps that there are many Filipinos in Queens. That's where I live. My brother-in-law—his name's Manjit—is dating a Filipina. Very pretty woman, nice and charming." He cleared his throat and said, *"Maganda ka. Iniibig kita."* You're beautiful. I love you. I glanced at the meter and saw it register $18.75.

"You say it almost like a native," I lied.

"Oh, thank you, thank you." He smiled gratefully. "So tell me, which hospital are you going to work for?"

"Hospital?"

"You are a nurse, aren't you? Or a doctor perhaps?"

"Sorry to disappoint you," I said. "So, how long have you been driving a taxi?"

"Not long really. Maybe four, five years. I don't do this full time. Another brother-in-law of mine and I run a fabric business in Jackson Heights. We sell very good Indian silks for saris, although we also import some from Japan and Hong Kong. But between you and me, they're definitely not the same quality."

"So why a cab?"

"Nowadays business is not so good. Not many people buying silks. Rayon and polyester are killing us."

Just then the meter registered $26.25, and he slowed to a stop at my mother's address. "We're here," he said cheerfully. After I paid him, he took out a calling card and handed it to me.

"When you're in the neighborhood, come by for a visit. I'll give you a very good price on a sari."

I threw the card away. Saris were not in my future.

I lingered on the sidewalk. Frankly, I was scared. My mother's building was a drab, nameless structure of washed-out limestone. Iron grilles on the ground-floor windows were like jagged teeth clenched together. There was graffiti on every inch of wall space, indecipherable wormlike scribbles and graphic representations. Did she have to put up with this every single day?

Directly across from the building were a small deli with posters selling Lotto, the *Daily News,* and Diet Pepsi; a Chinese takeout; an auto body shop; and a 24-hour Laundromat. A parking lot next to the Laundromat seemed to be the perfect place for dumping dead bodies. I smiled. I watched *Miami Vice* too much.

On the northwest corner of my mother's block were rows of attached houses with vinyl siding or red brick. Each of them had a small front porch where I could see elderly men and women reclined against their folding chairs. Clay-colored shingle rooftops and awnings in a variety of peppermint stripes were backdrops for neatly trimmed evergreen hedges and hydrangea bushes.

I felt a cool breeze wrap itself around my neck as cars drove by, loud Latin music emanating from their open windows. The elderly men and women slowly got up, collapsed their folding chairs, and went indoors. Lights began appearing in windows. It was probably dinnertime.

I pulled my suitcase up to the building's front landing and looked for my mother's name on the buzzer. It wasn't there. This couldn't be the wrong address. I had checked it with her twice. I quickly opened the secret flap of my wallet where I had taped her address to make sure I was in the right place. I was. I turned the doorknob a couple of times, but it wouldn't budge. There was a pay phone next to the deli, but right now a man was using it, his hands gesturing wildly, his voice screaming something unintelligible into the handset. I shuddered at the thought of using the same phone and having his saliva find its way into mine. The trouble one had to go through to get a cab ride, press a buzzer, see one's mother.

I ran a finger across the entire buzzer panel, pressing desperately on each button. The intercom crackled immediately with several voices talking at the same time. "Who is it?" said one, "Yes?" asked another, *"Que?"* barked a third. I said nothing until the sound of the voice I had heard only by phone for the last two years spoke to me.

"Sino?" my mother asked in Tagalog.

A loud buzz followed. As I pushed the door open, I heard footsteps scamper down the carpeted staircase. I had just stepped into the foyer when I saw my mother by the foot of the stairs, her eyes glistening with tears. The shock of seeing her after such a long time deleted any other memory I might have had of her. Her hair was much lighter than I had remembered it, and no longer lacquered with hairspray. She had put on weight—most of it flattering—and she was smiling. She was also wearing the colorful housedress I had sent her for her birthday.

I dropped my things to embrace her, but she was already dragging one of my suitcases up the stairs. As we walked up to her apartment, the walls resonated with her voice, summarizing her life in the three flights it took us to get there. She didn't ask about my flight or the taxi ride. She didn't even ask how I was.

"Oh, I'm so glad you're here, Viola," she sighed, as we stood just outside her door. She pulled a bunch of keys from her pocket and inserted them into three different locks.

"You look like St. Peter," I joked, but she didn't respond. She turned the knob sharply and jabbed the door with her knee.

I pulled my suitcase from behind, almost knocking off the vase on top of the television set as I walked in. My mother disappeared behind a wall.

"Make yourself at home," she shouted from the other side. "Sit down and relax. Turn on the TV if you want."

"Nice place you got, Mom," I shouted back, helping myself to one of the Godiva mint candies filling a ceramic bowl. I bit into one and immediately spit it out. It was moldy.

"What's that smell?" I asked.

"Our dinner," she laughed.

"No, not that. It doesn't smell like food, it smells like naph-thalene—"

"Oh, the moth balls. I have them everywhere."

"But you're not in Manila anymore."

"I know, but I just want to make sure that—" She stopped in mid-sentence, and I heard footsteps suddenly charging at me. As I turned around, I saw my mother down on her knees, urgently pulling at my shoes. *"Eeee!"* she shrieked. "This is a no-shoes apartment. It's hard vacuuming this place."

I mumbled an apology, which she didn't hear, and strolled around her studio, feeling my way into my mother's life. It was small and cramped, but decorated in such a way that no one would have noticed just how little of her world it contained.

There were two large windows on one side, where Roman shades in a plaid pattern of pastel peach and lime green hung halfway, and a matching sofa bed in the same color scheme right beneath them. The smell of freshly removed plastic was strong, and I saw a price tag hanging from the armrest. Resisting a look at the amount, I pulled it off and tore it into pieces.

In the middle of the room were a glass coffee table with a silk flower arrangement and a pair of large throw pillows on the floor. A daybed was off to the other side, next to a bistro table, a pair of matching chairs, and a black halogen floor lamp.

I saw the three bookcases she had put together, arranged at different points in her studio. Each shelf bulged with hardcover books, photo albums, manila envelopes, and folders marked "Utilities," "VISA," "Citibank statements," "Discount coupons."

Several shoe boxes overflowed with letters, all of them, as far as I could tell, mine. Resting on top of one bookcase was her statue of the Child Jesus of Prague, its beatific face reflecting the glow from the fluttering flames of the two votive candles by its feet.

On the wall above the daybed were a calendar from the St. Thomas Aquinas parish church, a Museum of Modern Art poster, and various photographs pinned with thumb tacks: my mother holding me when I was probably less than a year old, me looking grumpy on my very first day at school, my one and only piano recital at the Academy, Mom standing next to Dad as he received a plaque from Ferdinand and Imelda Marcos because our bookstore had donated its printing services to one of their pet projects, our house, my prom picture, her parents.

"Halika na, anak. Let's eat," she called out from the kitchen. I remembered the present I had brought all the way from Manila.

"What's that?" she asked, eyeing the jar I was holding.

"It's *burong mangga.* From our mango tree. I pickled them myself."

My mother's eyes lit up as she eagerly unscrewed the cap and reached in for a slice. "My God! You're lucky they didn't take this away from you at the airport," she said, sinking her teeth into a half-moon slice of the yellow-green fruit, its tart fragrance immediately filling the kitchen.

Then her forehead broke into fine pleats. "It's not sour enough. Never mind, I'll fix it later. Look, I've prepared your favorite *pochero* just as you like it." She placed the jar by the kitchen sink, next to the bottles of Ivory dishwashing liquid, Vaseline hand lotion, and an old yogurt container filled with pot scrubbers and an assortment of colored sponges.

She uncovered the casserole, releasing hot, steaming vapors of stewed plum tomatoes, pork *chorizo de bilbao,* chicken, green cabbage leaves, and potatoes.

"Since when did you learn how to cook?" I asked her.

"I just got tired of eating dried fish and fried Spam all the time. Dede introduced me to a Filipina who is the cook for the Spanish ambassador. I asked her to teach me some recipes. This is the *pochero* she prepares for the ambassador and his family. The woman's nice, but she's not in our class, if you know what I mean. She claims her family lives somewhere in Santa Mesa, but who knows, they could be anywhere in Blumentritt. I never even heard of the school she went to. It's funny because when we first met, she was overfriendly, asking me which part of Manila I came from, and what I used to do. When I told her, she suddenly backed off and refused to tell me anything more about herself. She knew there was no way she could keep her background from me. Anyway, whenever her employers are away on home leave, she invites her friends over and cooks for them. On my last birthday, she honored me with a dinner using the embassy crystal and china. I even got to sleep in the same bedroom where a daughter of King Juan Carlos once spent the night. *Sige na,* help yourself before it gets cold. I have *patis, toyo,* all the Filipino condiments I need. Some water?"

"I'm really not that hungry," I said, suddenly feeling weary.

But my mother blithely proceeded to dish out the *pochero* anyway, pouring me a glass of water. We sat across from each other silently, the sound of our silverware banging against our plates as we moved our food around.

"So tell me," she began, between nibbles of chicken, dipping a spoon into a saucer filled with fish sauce and sprinkling it on her rice, "was it difficult getting out of the country?"

"I was issued a passport in two days without any problem. The American consul reviewed all my documents and told me to pick up my visa the next day."

"I was worried that you'd also be on the travel ban because of your father."

"He's the one in trouble, not me."

She nodded thoughtfully. "We keep hearing all these horror stories about the U.S. Embassy in Manila. The most recent one was about a well-dressed lady who was denied a tourist visa without the benefit of an interview. The consular officer supposedly didn't even look at her stack of documents. He just stamped 'Denied' on her application form, and that was the end of that. The poor woman went berserk inside the embassy. She waved her papers at the officer and said, 'You didn't even look! You didn't even look!' She had to be escorted out by the embassy police. These consuls think they're better than God. If I were in her place, I probably would have lost it too. *Naku,* these *kanos* are just punishing us Filipinos for trying to get rid of the bases. It's a good thing I got mine through the embassy drop box. So how's Manila? It's amazing how Cory survives one coup after the other."

"She's a woman with nine lives."

"Is it true that the power interruptions have gotten worse?"

"Yes, but you learn to live with them."

"Thank God I live here. I never have to worry about blackouts or water shortages. If an appliance gets broken, I just throw it away and get myself a new one. You'll love the sales in this country! There's one every day. If I don't feel like cooking, I can always go to one of those Korean delis or a Taco Bell. I get around on the subway and never have to worry about traffic. There's twenty-four-hour cable TV, and I can watch everything there. After cable, who needs Carnegie Hall?"

We were quiet again as our conversation hit a dead end, the two of us strained, I suspected, by having to be daughter and mother to each other, roles that had been largely diminished by our time apart. I was no longer the adolescent she had left behind in Manila.

Would our reunion have been any easier if we were just two friends who hadn't seen each other in two years? Except my mother and I were not meeting as friends. We were stuck, whether we liked it or not, with a strict sense of hierarchy and seniority. That was how my mother was raised, that was how she expected to raise me.

How often I heard her say, "You are only my child; these are the rules of my house, my this, my that," so it was only natural for me to assume that I was nothing but an appendage of my mother, an extension of her body, if not of her being. Even when we *both* became victims of a marriage gone awry we could not alter our roles. We couldn't find comfort and solace in our mutual pain.

How could we be friends when friendship was between equals? *I was never hers.*

To my mother I was the child with dials and knobs, programmed to meet certain standards, guaranteed to bring about satisfactory results. No return, no exchange. I was free to express ideas and opinions so long as they echoed hers. Contradiction was met with censure that sometimes turned ugly, and when that wasn't enough, she would revert to her weapon of last resort: her authority over me, delivered with a resounding slap for good measure.

She was proud to show me off to her friends and relatives, constantly telling them how *nicely* I turned out despite everything that our family had become. I was reduced to a testament to her parenting skills, another figurine to display with the rest of her crystal collection.

For a while I had liked the attention and was flattered by

comparisons to her. *Like mother, like daughter* sustained me in dark moments of insecurity, restoring my faith in myself when I had lost the ability to believe. But all that changed when she left. *I* changed. Roles became less important, chronology belonged to a calendar, I was heady at the options available to me.

Now that we were both in America, could our shared experience of being foreigners in a country that wasn't ours be our second chance to find the common thread between us, outside of being just mother and child to each other? Could our sense of isolation from what was safe and familiar be reduced by our being together? Or were we doomed to spend the rest of our lives tallying up our differences, keeping a scorecard of our failures simply because we couldn't let go of the roles we were each born into?

As I sat and looked at my mother, I couldn't imagine telling her *my* story. Could I tell her about the nights *yaya* had to sleep with me because I was afraid I might never wake up? Or the times I'd scream for her because I had dreamed that she had died in a plane crash. How could I tell her that I had always missed her? Or ask, *Why did you leave me?*

When we spoke again, it was easier for us to retreat into the neutral conversation about her friends in Manila ("Are so-and-so still married?" "I heard so-and-so bought a co-op on Fifth Avenue," "Which monopoly is so-and-so in control of now?") whose lives I couldn't care less about; the people she read about in the tabloids; the performances she had watched on television; the investments she had made, although when I asked her if they were in treasury bills or treasury bonds, she immediately changed the subject.

"By the way, you never told me where you ended up working after you left Flescher and Simmons," I said finally.

My mother stood up, gathered our plates, and arranged them

in a neat pile next to the sink. She squeezed a few drops of lotion onto the palm of her hand, rubbed it vigorously into her skin, and slipped on a pair of yellow latex gloves. I also got up from my seat. As the steam from the running hot water draped itself around my mother's fingers, I cleared the table of debris.

"I work as a housekeeper on the Upper East Side."

I turned around to face her. "Excuse me?"

Without turning around, she repeated, "I'm a housekeeper."

"You're a maid?"

"In America, they—we—are called housekeepers."

"Same thing. Since when?"

She was now cleaning the rice cooker, vigorously scouring the burned portions at the bottom as if that singular act would obliterate the impact of what she had become.

"Shortly after the Malixi thing. Ever since Reagan signed that immigration bill, employers ask for proof that you can legally work in this country. I couldn't find anyone to sponsor me. I had no qualifications. As a housekeeper, nobody asks such questions, and I'm paid off the books."

"Does anyone else know?"

"Only my close friends. I always tell others I sell life insurance."

"You came to America to work as a maid?"

She shut off the faucet and faced me, her gloved hands wrapped in giant bubbles dripping on the floor. "Don't be so pompous! I'm not begging for money. I'm not prostituting myself. I never asked you for money, did I? Did I?"

I shook my head. "But a maid—"

"So what? In America nobody cares what you do for a living. A lot of *pinoys* do it, including ex-engineers and teachers in Manila. Even Ph.D.s work as taxi drivers. At least here, they treat you with dignity and you have days off."

"Do you wear a uniform?"

"Only when the Steinbergs—they're my employers—have company. It's all black except for the white apron, which has eyelet on the border."

"This is why you came to America?"

This is what she left me for?

She turned her back on me and continued to wash the dishes. She told me to take the mop next to the refrigerator and dry the floor. I'd never used one before. Barely concealing her exasperation, she said, "Viola, wake up!" She got the mop herself and wiped the floor dry. She was quick and good at it. Not one spot left behind when she was done. Was this what she looked like when she worked? She went to a brown paper bag filled with garbage and threw in more trash. She folded the top over and told me to bring it down to the sidewalk where the building's garbage cans were.

"You should come one day and meet Elfrida," she said, just before I walked out with the trash.

"Elfrida?" I asked.

"That's Mrs. Steinberg. I never call her that to her face, naturally. That wouldn't be polite."

I was back on the same sidewalk I had stood on a few hours before. Nothing had changed. The same stores, the same hubcaps, the same *boom-boom* from passing cars, probably even the same laundry being hauled in and out. I looked up to the sky and saw no stars, no clouds. It lacked the rich texture of velvet; it was black and flat.

At least in Manila the skies were never like this, not even when the weather was in transition. There was always something going on. Thunder. Lightning. Stars elbowing each other for more room. Clouds meandering about as if all they ever did was listen to Debussy. Here, they were just pale blotches of condensed water. I bet New Yorkers never get a full moon the way we do in Manila. There are too many things obscuring their view.

When I returned to the apartment, I found my mother in the bathroom flossing her teeth. As she moved the string to and fro between her molars, she said, "I'm surprised Caloy hasn't called. I thought that the reason you didn't want me to meet you at the airport was because he was going to be there."

"Drive all the way from Cambridge to meet me at the airport? I told him we'd get together as soon as I settled down."

"I think he's serious about you, Viola."

"Mom—"

"Okay, okay. You'll like living in New York once you get used to it. You're lucky I arrived here first. I had no one except your *tita* Dede. That sofa bed is for you. I got that and the matching shades on sale just two weeks ago. I've also cleared out half of my closet for your clothes. Hmm, we may need more space for your winter stuff. Oh, never mind. Once we can afford it, we can move into a bigger apartment. We don't have to live in Queens, you know. We can find one in the city if you like."

"I don't intend to live here permanently," I said, but she didn't hear me.

Then, as she switched off the bathroom lights and walked to her bed, she added, "You must be exhausted."

"It was a long trip," I said lamely, noticing that in my brief absence, she had gotten the sofa bed ready for me. I changed into a T-shirt and slid underneath the comforter. I turned on my side and looked at my mother just as she finished making the Sign of the Cross.

"Are you happy?" I asked her.

"Of course," she said as she reached above her head to turn off the light. "At least I work on the Upper East Side."

23

I could not sleep. The apartment felt odd and strange. Lying there on my bed, the entire room seemed to be shrinking inch by inch, closing in on me. The mattress springs bore deep into my flesh, the air was thick and heavy. In the darkness I felt the footsteps of my nightmares marching back into my life, ready to take over.

There was my father, mocking the people who always walked around with an outstretched hand, expecting to be on the receiving end of someone else's benevolence, including God's. "Give me this, give me that," I could hear him saying, "as if all God ever did was answer prayers and make miracles." I saw him ridicule the poor because all they ever did was beg.

There was my hand, the veins large and warped, writing "Maid" in the space reserved for occupation, writing "TNT" for immigration status. Again and again my hand wrote, each stroke bigger and bolder for everyone to see, my fingers unable to stop the truth from announcing itself.

Then everything went dark. I forced the images to return, but they came back only in trickles. Like the day I came home from school and saw my parents' bedroom door slightly open, a silent invitation for me to walk in. It was shortly after three, so I knew that my mother had to be taking her afternoon *siesta*. My father rarely came home before five. I stopped right by the door.

There was my father standing behind my mother, his trousers and underpants all the way down to the floor; she was lying on her stomach by the edge of the bed, the hem of her dress raised above her waist. The veins on his arms seemed to explode as he gripped her shoulders. There was no sound from either of them, only the faint rustle of bedsheets. Why was he standing that way? What was he *doing* to my mother? Why was he hurting her? My mother's face was resting on its side, her cheeks bunched up from the pressure of my father's body. Then he heaved and slumped on top of her.

The floor creaked. My mother turned toward me. I screamed. I opened my eyes and looked around, finding comfort at the sight of the walls flooded with abstract murals of light and shadow. I heard the wall clock mark time, the lonely wail of a siren speeding through the night. I felt the earth shiver each time the train rumbled by.

Then I saw my mother, sleeping as she always did, her body curled up like a snail around a pillow, squeezing it.

I'm a housekeeper. I'm a housekeeper. Her revelation left me cold and empty. And then to say that she was happy because she worked on the Upper East Side.

I got up from my bed and tiptoed to her side, careful not to wake her. I knelt and put my cheek on hers. What dreams did she have in the inner recesses of her mind? When my father left, I used to sneak into her room while she was asleep and hold my hand inches above her face, waiting for the gentle drift of her breath to come to me. Making sure that she hadn't lost consciousness in the middle of the night.

I returned to my bed and pulled the covers up to my chin,

surrendering to the pleasure of being wrapped among its folds. I hadn't been here for twenty-four hours, yet the Philippines seemed to be light years away. When I turned to look out the window, I noticed that there was a full moon obscured by clouds. That wasn't a good sign.

2 4

For the next week and a half, I was barely coherent, floating in and out of jet lag. This despite all we had to say to one another. My mother took time off to be with me, incurring, I could tell, the displeasure of Mrs. Steinberg, who didn't mince words over the phone, saying that she expected longer hours *without pay* in return. I had to turn my eyes away from my mother; I couldn't stand listening to her. I couldn't stand this Mrs. Steinberg.

I really wouldn't have minded if my mother had to work, considering that I was useless most of the time anyway, but she was eager to mother me, to show me the city. She wanted to show me all that she had learned since she moved to America, to let me see that she had survived. But almost always, just when we were about to walk out the door, the exhaustion would suddenly hit me, and I would find myself back in bed. On the one day that we finally did manage to go out, we went to see the Statue of Liberty. I was suddenly hit by a severe case of vertigo, and on the ferry back to Manhattan, I got so seasick I had to spend another day in bed.

Sometimes I thought that she was not the mother I remembered. That one seemed more dependent, given to melodrama, self-indulgent. That one was burdened by an unwanted marriage. A martyr. This one, on the other hand, was self-assured, independent. I detected an inner strength that was never there before. She cooked all our meals, bought the groceries, took care of the laundry, and balanced her checkbook all by herself. She was now taking charge of her life instead of merely reacting to it. But I also detected something else: a cynicism that gave that strength a brittle edginess. I didn't know which mother I liked better; I didn't think that, either way, I had much of a choice.

My mother refused all offers of help from me, including help with the dishes. "Are you afraid that I'm going to break your china?" I asked one time as we stood by the sink, the two of us tugging and pulling at a platter that eventually slipped and crashed to the floor. When I offered to share with her some of the money that my father had given me, she was so offended she refused to speak to me for a day. "How could you?" she said tearfully as I tried to explain that I only wanted to help out. "You insult my home," she said.

When she began talking to me again, the first thing she did was apologize for the dreary appearance of the apartment. "Wouldn't it be nice to have fresh flowers instead of these fake ones," she sighed. She reminded me to take extra precautions when using the toilet, because the paint was peeling from the seat cover, and she didn't want scratch marks all over my behind. Little by little she began to give labels to the dreariness of her life. So that when I came home one day holding a dozen white gladiolas in my arms, purchased from a florist and not from a corner deli, my mother excitedly grabbed them and arranged them in the new glass vase I had also bought, singing happily to herself. She didn't rebuke me for the extravagance.

Living together became a lot easier after that, but it wasn't always peaceful. We never talked about money again and pursued our household chores with equal diligence, but there were times when the apartment was like an army barracks, and she was my drill sergeant. Our conversations became a series of one-sided lectures.

"You know," she would say, "when Americans think of illegal aliens, they think of the farm hands and the gardeners in jobs they themselves wouldn't be caught dead doing. The ones who dash across the border, crawl under wire fences. But look at me. I look even more corporate than some of those personnel executives who don't deserve to clean my bathroom. And they have the nerve to tell me that I can't work for them. The assholes!"

I had never heard my mother utter a curse word before. Now they were her second language.

My mother had a point, but I didn't need to hear it as often as she drummed it into my head. She was really trying to convince herself. But how could I tell her that I didn't want to go to bed each night wondering if she was still going to be here the next morning? I didn't want to jump every time there was a knock on the door, or hide her in the utility closet, or look behind me every time I thought someone might be following us. Following her. There were enough muggers in the city; I didn't need to have other distractions as well.

"Whether this country is willing to accept it or not," she was saying, "illegal aliens have always been a part of its history. That's what happens when one country is rich and another is poor. Did the Native Americans turn away the Pilgrims when they first arrived? Did the natives say, 'Sorry, no vacancy'? Why was it okay to come in then, and it isn't now?"

It was hard to talk to my mother, especially when she assumed that having stayed in this country for so long meant that she was untouchable. I didn't want to talk about illegal aliens anymore. It was one thing to *know* an illegal alien. Another to *live* with one.

We were on our second helpings of ice cream when she yawned and said, "We need to get you a Social Security number. You can't do anything in this country without it, not even die! We'll also get you a driver's license. I hope you remembered to bring your Philippine one as I told you to."

"I did, but I haven't driven in a long time."

"That doesn't matter. You need it only for identification."

"Do I have to take an exam?"

"Only a written one, and it's multiple choice. All you have to do is show them your passport and a valid Philippine driver's license. Once you pass, you'll have your New York City license."

"What about an immigration lawyer? Shouldn't I see one as soon as possible?"

My mother's body stiffened, and she rose abruptly, walked to the bathroom, and shut the door behind her. After a few moments, I heard the door open, and I got up and joined her. She was standing over the sink, stretching one side of her forehead upward, plucking her few remaining eyebrows with a tweezer. I leaned against the doorway and waited. Anything else might set her off.

"Lawyer for what?"

"My papers."

She pinched herself with the tweezer and stopped what she was doing. "I'm sorry. I forget that you're an FOJ."

"A what?"

"Fresh Off the Jet. Lawyers are only interested in the green stuff inside your wallet. People like you are every immigration lawyer's pot of gold at the end of the rainbow."

"You said that all I needed was to get here and everything would fall into place. Daddy said you'd take care of everything."

"Don't get hysterical. Of course I'll take care of it. I just don't see the rush. It's not like the INS is knocking on our door."

"I don't want to have the INS knocking on our door. I don't want to be a—" I stopped and looked at her.

"Go ahead," she said quietly. "Say it. TNT. You don't want to be a TNT."

"Don't you want to be legal?"

"I pay my taxes, I stay out of trouble, I'm not on welfare. What more could anyone want?"

"But your name isn't even on the buzzer."

"Please, Viola, get real. Do you know how lucky you and I are that we even got into this country? I've served my time. And now you want to throw that away because of some technicality? So see a lawyer. They'll tell you the same story and bleed you dry."

"I didn't come here to live like that. I didn't come here to lie."

"So why did you come? What were you thinking when I arranged for your father to send you? So that we could go shopping at Macy's?"

Because I wanted to be with you, my head screamed at her.

"How can you lie all the time?" I cried.

"The trick is keeping ahead of the lie. You're only as good as your last lie. Look at me. Look how long I've lasted."

"But you've only been here two years."

"Who's counting? Endurance is the trademark of a good liar. After a while, it becomes automatic. You don't even think about it."

"But you feel trapped. It's claustrophobic."

"Maybe for you. Not for me."

"What about going back?"

"To the heat? The dust? Your father and his women? No thanks. I'll leave when I'm good and ready, unless someone decides to turn me in." She stopped and looked at me. "It's really not all that difficult. You'll get used to it."

Not me. Never me.

25

It took me several months to finally adjust and make the transition from the life I had had in Manila to the life I was about to have, no matter how temporary, here in New York. Sometimes the adjustment had the feel of sitting back against an easy chair, my feet up on the footstool, expecting all the pieces to fall into place. But there were times when I couldn't help but feel that my life was on a holding pattern. Forever. That was too much of a burden to contemplate.

One evening, shortly after my mother returned home from work, she dropped several brochures and catalogues on my lap. They were from schools like New York University's School of Continuing Education, Parson's, The New School, Fashion Institute of Technology, and the French Culinary Institute. I found that last one a particularly odd choice considering that I could barely make rice. Besides, why would I want to learn how to cook French food when I couldn't even pronounce a fraction of what I was supposed to be making?

I ended up enrolling in a couple of business courses at NYU, including a class in public speaking just for the heck of it.

School was infinitely better than staying home and listening to my mother talk about the pillows she fluffed every day, the *whatshisname*—Muffy? Buffy?—dog she walked, the art books she dusted and arranged in alphabetical order. Once, when I excitedly described to her a class discussion on downsizing municipal government through privatization, she only sat still and looked straight ahead at me with a dull, sightless stare.

Cecilia and Libeth wrote me often. Libeth even teased in one of her letters that Pasig was not the same since I left. I missed my friends. I missed my house. I even missed having Eladio drive for me. I kept reminding myself, as I looked around at my classmates with their pierced navels and ripped jeans, their heads filled with ideas that were alien to me, that I wasn't going to be here for a long time. I wished my father would finally call and say that it was safe to go back home, but he never did.

For no matter how much I tried, I found it hard to concentrate. I couldn't get my mother's status out of my mind. The longer I stayed, the more determined I became to prove my mother wrong. I was sure that sooner or later, I could help her.

Al Borotto's advertisement in *Pinoy Weekly* called him an immigration specialist and added in bold, black letters, "FREE CONSULTATION." Without telling my mother, I skipped a class and went to see him.

Fulton Street between Broadway and Nassau was a narrow spit of filth crowded with stores. When Al Borotto said that he worked "in the Wall Street area," I had had an image of tall glass buildings, money, and expensively dressed men and women. I had no idea that "the Wall Street area" was a wider expanse than his statement had implied, or that his office was nowhere near where he would have people believe it was.

I walked up and down Fulton street looking for his address,

knocking against empty soda cans, stepping on burning cigarette butts. I was frightened by the quick-stepping yuppies who brushed past me, their cellular phones pressed against their ears.

Borotto's address turned out to be wedged between a hot dog–falafel stand and an instant-photo place. His nameplate wasn't on the building's wall directory, but the elevator creaked up to the fifth floor. As I entered his office, I was disappointed by the man who greeted me. Al Borotto was tired and disheveled. I should have realized at once that he was not the kind of lawyer I had in mind, but it was too late to back out.

His office was small and stuffy, dense with cigarette smoke. Numerous folders teetered on top of his desk while grubby leather-bound books filled bookshelves made of laminated wood.

"So what do you want?" he asked, linking his hands together on top of a writing pad.

I was suddenly nervous. Shit, I was betraying my mother!

"It's rather complicated. It's for someone I know. She needs a work permit."

"What's her visa?"

"Tourist."

"How long has she been here?"

"Almost three years."

He laughed long and loud. "You expect me to help your friend after three years? What has your friend been doing? Hanging out in Atlantic City?"

"Perhaps I should leave," I said and began to gather my things.

"Sit down!" he blasted, rising halfway from his seat. "I just found that funny. What are her skills? Don't lie."

I shrugged my shoulders. "She's always been a housewife."

He raised his right hand to his chin and began stroking it absentmindedly.

"But she's a college graduate," I said quickly.

"And so are eight thousand other people—some of them even have MBAs."

"Can you help my friend?"

"If I can't, nobody can. I wish you had come to me sooner; we would have had more time to put things together for the INS. I don't understand why people are so afraid of the INS."

"Well, nobody wants to be deported."

"Don't interrupt! There is a difference between the *letter* of the law and the *spirit* of the law. The spirit of the law—ah, this is the beauty of what I do for a living"—he struck his index finger against his temple—"is getting into the soul of that law. Why was it written in the first place? What is the bottom line?"

From a drawer, he took out a thick folder marked "Testimonials" and placed it on my lap. "Read!" he commanded.

Inside were letters from Borotto's satisfied clients, all typed under his letterhead in a strikingly uniform typeface.

"I may have an ugly office," Borotto continued, "but I get things done. Why should anyone go to a big-time law firm when I can do the same thing for a quarter of what they charge? I get them all: Irish, Hispanic, Polish, Pakistani. Do you follow me?"

"Yes, but you still haven't answered my question."

"I'm getting there. First of all, I want to meet this friend of yours, to make sure that this is not a phantom case. Does she have money?"

"You don't have to worry about that," I assured him, hurriedly placing the testimonial folder on his Out tray.

Suddenly he asked, "Which part of the Philippines are you from?"

"Manila."

"Quezon City, Caloocan, Forbes Park, Dasmariñas, Bel Air?"

Before I could give him an answer, he suddenly slammed a

fist on his desk. "Isn't America something? You Manila folk with your fancy cars, exclusive subdivisions, and five-star hotels end up with a lawyer like me. You probably even went to a convent school, didn't you?"

"What *province* do you come from?" I asked.

His pseudo-American accent didn't fool me. It could not disguise his provincial beginnings. I was sure he was from the part of the Philippines where roads and highways were nothing more than election campaign promises that have yet to be delivered. Where Madonna was still known as the Mother of Jesus. For a country boy, he had some nerve.

"Actually," he said, "I grew up in the tobacco fields of San Isidro, Ilocos Norte, attended public school there, and went to Manila on a scholarship from the Lyceum. Have you ever been up north?"

"No reason to. So when did you come to the United States?"

"Twenty years ago. All my kids—I have five—were born here. Three of them drive their own cars."

"Have you been back?"

"Oh, the *missis* and I try to visit every two years—my mother still lives there—but it's getting harder and harder to make that long a trip. What about you, where's the rest of your family?"

"I'm an only child. My father lives in Manila. I live with my mother in Queens. They—my parents—recently separated."

"Is your mother the *she* who needs help?"

I nodded.

Borotto clicked his tongue. I could tell he was savoring the information. "I can arrange a divorce if you like. We can even work out a package deal with the divorce and your mother's work permit. What about your visa?"

"Mine's fine. I don't intend to make America my home."

"Just asking. With regard to your mother, she's been here so long, we need to work a little harder. Doesn't she just want to remain a TNT? After three years, it almost doesn't pay to—"

"I don't want her to."

"Well, we need to find an employer who will be willing to sponsor her. To be honest, with unemployment so high and the labor force in excess, companies are not in the mood to deal with legal hassles unless you're Einstein reincarnated."

"There has to be some way."

"Of course, once we arrange a divorce she can also enter into an arranged marriage, but considering her recent experience, I doubt she'll go for it. Besides, I heard that the going rate is now five thousand, in cash. And that's if you marry a black. Whites charge slightly higher."

"Is the citizenship any different? Do they have to live together?"

"The INS goes to the extent of interviewing neighbors, inspecting the place of cohabitation. They're especially suspicious of crosscultural marriages, like a *pinoy* marrying a black. Once they find out, it's out the door immediately."

"So, what else can we do?"

"Perhaps your mother can set up her own business."

"My family owns a bookstore in Manila."

"Did you just say bookstore? Are you related to the Dacanay of the famous bookstore?"

"That's us."

"My goodness. I used to go there for my schoolbooks when it was still in the *bodega*. I remember the old man who owned the place. I was too poor to pay, so he'd always let me pay later. What was his name again?"

"Deogracias. My grandfather."

"That's it! How is he by the way?"

"He died a long time ago. So tell me about setting up the business."

"I'm afraid that's not covered by my free consultation. Why don't we talk about this some other day?"

He pushed back against his desk and stood up.

"But you said we don't have that much time."

Borotto walked back to his desk and said, "If you want more details, you'll have to pay my consultation fee."

"How much?"

"For today, two hundred fifty. All other visits will cost you one twenty-five an hour. Cash."

I took out the money and put it on his desk. He instantly became friendlier.

"*Bueno.* Your father," he began as he quickly pocketed my money, "who is, I assume, the CEO in the Philippines, will write a letter appointing your mother as the U.S.-based president of Galaxy Books. In this capacity, she is authorized to open a branch in New York City, where many Filipinos live. We'll submit financial statements showing that your father, or the company, has at least one million dollars in capital to invest in the branch. We will then be able to apply for a trader's visa on that basis."

"Will this visa allow her to seek employment?"

"Technically, no. The idea is that she is her own employer."

"So why would she want this visa if she can't go and find a job with it?"

"Weren't you listening to what I said? This visa will legalize her stay. She can go in and out of the country. She can apply for a Social Security card that will allow her to work. Speaking of which, do you know if she still has her I-94?"

"What is that?"

"The white card Immigration gives you at the time you enter this country. Does she still have it?"

"I'm not sure."

"Make sure. Otherwise, she may have to leave and come in again. I don't want to risk that and get her denied at the port of entry. Of course, there's always Canada."

"Have you ever done this before?"

He cleared his throat again. "Frankly, no, but my colleagues have, and it's worked for their clients."

"Can somebody else in the company do the authorization besides my father?"

"It was that bad? Well, as long as you can get blank letterheads of the company leave the rest to me. Nobody will ever know whose signature appears on the appointment letter anyway. But what about the company's financial statements?"

"I can ask my father's office to send me a copy."

"Good, good. We can even show that since the bookstore is essentially a Filipino enterprise serving the Filipino community, it needs to hire Filipino employees from the motherland. If we do that, you can even bring in a maid for your personal use and no one will ever know whether she works in the bookstore or in your apartment. To further impress the INS, we'll say that we are hiring locally as a way of reducing unemployment. They'll love that. Imagine a foreigner from a Third World country boosting the local economy."

"How much will you charge for all of this?"

"You shouldn't think of it in terms of how much you're going to spend."

"How much?"

"It's what happens in the end that matters."

"How much?"

"Well, this is just an estimate, it could go higher, it could go lower—"

"Mr. Borotto—"

"Around three thousand—"

"Three—what!?"

"In honor of your grandfather's memory and his many kindnesses to me, I will let you pay in installments. No other law firm will do that for you. All of them ask for fifty percent down and full payment in the end. I'll just ask a thousand up front to pay for the initial paperwork. For the rest I can just draw up an easy payment plan. You know, hire now, pay later."

"Can you guarantee it will work?"

"On the heads of my grandchildren."

"But what if it doesn't?"

The phone rang just then, and he excused himself to answer it. After he hung up, I told him that I needed to think about it a little more, and I'd get back to him.

As I walked out, he warned, "Don't wait too long. And bring your mother next time. I'd love to meet her."

· · ·

"TANGA!" my mother screamed at me when I told her what I had done. "How could you have been so stupid? Borotto never passed the bar in the Philippines. The man isn't even licensed to practice in the U.S."

"His ad said free, so I went."

"Stupidity is the second leading cause of death in this country, Viola, next to heart disease. Nothing is free in this country."

"I was only trying to help."

"And now see what's happened to you. How much did Borotto get you for?"

"How does he get away with it?"

"That's what happens when your clients are illegal."

"But he said that his clients weren't just *pinoys*. He had Pakistanis, Canadians, Po—"

"Did you think that only Filipinos are illegal aliens? This is America. But Borotto's smart, make no mistake. He employs a bona fide retired lawyer who makes all the court appearances and signs all the legal documents. You never get to see Borotto's signature. He works behind the scenes and handles all the administrative details."

"So why hasn't anyone turned him in?"

"For being a capitalist? Do you honestly think that a TNT will call the police? Borotto could make a killing with the INS if he wanted to by reporting all the names in his Rolodex."

"How do you know?"

"I went to him twice, shortly after I arrived. Like you, I saw his ad, went to his office. When I realized what he was doing— did he make you read his testimonials?—I refused to go back. After all the money I paid him, he never lifted a finger to get my papers fixed. He even lost my I-94. Then he threatened to report me. My God, I hope you didn't give him this address! Does he have this phone number?"

"No, he doesn't."

"Now you've lost your money. I thought you'd be a lot smarter than that."

"It's only money."

"Why can't you just leave things as they are, Viola? Just let me be. I am happy. Truly happy."

I didn't believe her.

26

I held the five-by-seven invitation card next to the *capiz* shell lamp and read aloud: *"The Asosasiyon ng mga Perlas ng Silangan, East Coast Chapter, cordially invites you to the* **Coronation of Ms. Pearl of the Orient–U.S.A.** *on Saturday, November 12. Dinner and dance to follow with music by the fantastic D' Fab 5 direct from Jersey City. Please keep the stub of your invitation for fabulous raffle prizes. Your taxable donation of $75 will benefit the typhoon victims of the Parish of Our Lady of Victory in Imus, Cavite."*

Farther down the card, in embossed gold letters, were the names of a Dr. Luzviminda Palaypay and a Dr. Ezequiel Parungao, the pageant's chairperson and vice-chairperson respectively. As chairperson of the pageant, Dr. Palaypay was called Queen of the Little Pearls.

I turned the card over and looked at her photograph sitting in a make-believe oyster throne, surrounded by the members of her court: South Sea Pearl, Baroque Pearl, Mabe Pearl, Majorica Pearl, and Mikimoto Pearl. They all looked the same to me: ear-to-ear smiles that must have taken months to practice, bouffant hairdos kept in place by rhinestone tiaras, and fully beaded strapless gowns that kept them from floating up to the sky. They were symbols of the successful immigrant. The provincial maiden gone stateside.

I felt a tug on my sleeve. Chinggay was offering me a glass of Coke. Dede, my mother, and I were in her Jersey City apartment on Henderson Street where, from the balcony of her fifteenth-floor studio, we could see the Manhattan skyline looking like metallic spears aimed at the sky.

This was the first time since I arrived that I had met my mother's friends. I hadn't wanted to go at first, but my mother insisted. "These are my oldest friends. You'll like them," she said. I saw that she was going to take it as a personal affront if I stayed behind. Anyway, it might be interesting to see if I could find out, through them, what my mother was like before I was born, when she still had her so-called sense of humor.

As I walked into Chinggay's apartment, she and Dede *ooh*ed and *aah*ed over how grown-up I looked, how poised, how more like a New Yorker than any of them. I was polite and gracious, and I could tell that my mother was pleased.

The only time I frowned was when Dede told me that I looked just like my mother when she was my age. I wasn't aware that I frowned until my mother brought it up on our way home. "I saw that face," she said. "What's wrong with being compared to me? I wasn't all that bad-looking, you know."

"Come on, Ludy, let's go," Chinggay was saying now as she stood by the kitchen sink, ferociously chopping a salad of green mango, onions, and tomatoes. We had brought grilled pork chops for dinner; they were sitting inside the microwave, waiting to be heated. Dede was setting the table.

"Why should we waste our time on a beauty contest?" my mother asked. "We know that *beauty* has nothing to do with it."

"I don't have a problem with parents who spend their money on raffle tickets just so they can claim that their daughter is a

Miss Something!" Dede said. "I can think of worse extrava-gances."

"Well, it certainly won't be at *my* expense. I never went to a beauty pageant in the Philippines and I'm not about to begin now," my mother declared.

"What a snob!" Dede said.

"Don't you want to take a break from living in America and pretend that we're back in the Philippines?" Chinggay asked.

"People party differently in America, you know," Dede observed.

"I'm sure they do, but I don't need to spend seventy-five dollars to find out. I could use some of that donation myself!"

"Is that what you're worried about?" Chinggay said. "I'll take care of it. I'll put the tickets down as a business expense. You know, part of my PR."

"Since when did you know about public relations?"

"There's nothing like a recession to learn new things, my dear."

"If you want to go that badly you should just go, Chinggay. Take Dede! Maybe Viola would want to join you too."

"No way!" I said. "If I go, *you're* coming along too." I was curious to see how *pinoys* partied in New York. Something new to write Cecilia about.

"I'll be honest with you," Chinggay said. "One of the girls is the daughter of a woman who bought life insurance from me and has been very helpful with leads and referrals."

"Ah, now the truth comes out. If—and that's a big if—we go with you, what's in it for us?" my mother asked.

"Stop being so difficult!" Chinggay replied sharply. "Is it because you're a TNT?"

I looked at my mother, who replied tartly, "While you're at

it, why don't you stand on your balcony and broadcast it to the rest of the world?"

"Oh, Chinggay, go to your coronation and leave us alone," Dede said impatiently.

Chinggay finished her chopping in silence. Dede shot me a warning glance. I walked to the TV and turned it on to *The Cosby Show*. Dede sat next to me, a bowl of potato chips on her lap. Chinggay scooped the salad into a serving bowl, threw a spoonful of shrimp paste into the mixture and stirred.

My mother broke the silence. "What if someone recognizes me?"

"Who cares?" Chinggay said.

"And they ask how long I've been in the United States, or which part of the Philippines I'm from, or if I'm a citizen or a green card holder."

"It's a little too late to feel paranoid." Dede yawned from the sofa.

Chinggay continued, "Say you're a citizen, and quickly change the subject. Once you put them on the defensive, they usually stop bothering you."

"But you know *pinoys*. They want to know everything, including how much money you have. My God, suppose I meet someone who knew Dado and me—forget it, I'm not going!"

Dede put the TV on mute and said, "Unless Manila finds out that Donald Trump has dumped Ivana to marry you, I don't think anyone will give a hoot about your life in New York. Dado's troubles will keep them busy for now."

"What's the latest on him?" Chinggay asked.

My mother looked at me. I told them what I knew.

"You're not actually worried about him, are you?" Dede asked my mother. "If I were in Cory's place, I would create presidential order three-oh-one, decreeing that Dado and others like him surrender their balls to the guillotine."

"I'd think Cory would be more concerned with finding out the true masterminds of her husband's assassination."

"Maybe Dado did it." Dede laughed.

"How much longer can his suspension last?" Chinggay asked.

"When I left," I said, "the PCGG was still collecting evidence against Tee Pak Long. Until they can clear and absolve Dad of any wrongdoing, the Board will continue to run Galaxy."

"Sounds like delaying tactics—" Chinggay began.

"—or perhaps it's time Dado paid off the right people," countered Dede.

"Dado wouldn't do that. He's too cheap!" my mother said.

"Why don't *you* go home and run the company yourself?" Dede said. "Wouldn't that just be the perfect revenge? After all, the bookstore belongs to you, not to him. I can see Dado crawling on his knees, begging for your favor!"

"Quit it, Dede," Chinggay said. "Let's eat!"

My mother smiled. I could tell that she liked Dede's idea.

$\bullet \ \bullet \ \bullet$

Two days later, all four of us arrived at Lakambini Restaurant in Flushing where a giant streamer on the canvas awning announced the Ms. Pearl of the Orient–U.S.A. pageant.

As I stood next to the plate-glass window and peered between the gaps in the vertical blinds hanging down the other side, I felt the heavy beat of the music pound on my chest. I saw men and women spin around the dance floor, the disco lights bouncing off their tuxedos and beaded gowns, leaving streaks of greens, violets, and reds as they moved from place to place.

Chinggay nudged me through the revolving door into the

ballroom, where a Philippine flag was standing next to a life-size portrait of President Corazon Aquino. The room resonated with the sounds of Tagalog, English, and other Philippine dialects. My mother kept mumbling about how familiar everyone looked. It was a typical TNT symptom.

I almost fainted from the overpowering scents of Aramis and Giorgio mingling with the aromas of roast garlic, *patis,* sugar-cane vinegar, roast pig, and San Miguel beer. A wave of home-sickness engulfed me.

It was wrong of my mother to assume that if she lived in this country long enough, she would become one of its own. Illegal, yes, but American nevertheless. The narratives she had invented for herself had nothing to do with who she was. How much longer could she keep up this self-deception?

Chinggay walked ahead of us, dropping a hello here, a quick introduction there. I didn't remember any of the names or faces we met. I was anxious for my mother; her fear of being recog-nized was getting to me. When nothing happened, I was much relieved and mildly disappointed.

Our reserved table was next to the carpeted runway that jutted out from the center stage. A ceremonial throne sat in the middle of a giant oyster shell painted in iridescent aqua and gold. Ripples of tinfoil covered the huge backdrop where clear plastic balls hung like water bubbles. Above the stage hung a pair of gaudy-looking mermaids, each of them holding one end of a streamer emblazoned with the pageant title.

We settled into our seats and pretended to look busy and engrossed in conversation. A waiter appeared with our compli-mentary drinks. When he left, Chinggay motioned for us to look casually to our right.

"Well, if it isn't George Davila. He owned that famous beauty parlor in Mandaluyong, remember?"

"Salon de Ylang-Ylang. But what name did he go by then?" my mother asked.

"He called himself Georgette!" Dede said.

"What's he doing here? Does he have a salon in New York?"

Chinggay came closer to us. "I have some gossip for you," she whispered. "I was on Fifth Avenue one day, and I saw Georgette, excuse me, George, coming out of the Vidal Sassoon salon. I was so excited to see an old friend that I waved frantically at him. He stopped and looked around. I shouted, 'Salon de Ylang-Ylang,' because surely he would know that. He finally looked across and saw me. But he just stood there, staring at me, as if he didn't know who I was. Screw him! I used to give him hundred peso tips. I even introduced him to this nephew of mine who eventually became his lover. I decided that I wasn't going to let him get away that easily. So I ran up to him and said, 'It's me, Chinggay Valencia.' He still pretended not to know me. So I said, 'Boyet—that's my nephew—misses you.' You should have seen his face. He realized he couldn't get away from me anymore, so he started screaming in excitement in the middle of Fifth Avenue."

We looked back at Georgette, standing serenely under a chandelier, holding a drink, his hair pulled tightly back into a ponytail. Under his left arm was a man's lizard clutch bag. Two elderly women hovered around him, and he leaned over to kiss one woman's cheek while he fussed over the other's pageboy. Then he greeted some passerby, his jeweled fingers waving as if he were royalty.

"Was he working at Vidal Sassoon's?" I asked. My mother threw me a sharp look. I had no right to insert myself in this conversation. They were her friends. Not mine.

"That's what I asked him. He didn't answer at first, so I asked again. His face suddenly tightened. Then he became defensive.

He said he used to work there, but not anymore. Now he and a Japanese partner were setting up their own salon, and he was trying to pirate a few of his former colleagues at Vidal's. He even told me to send him anyone I know."

"What was unusual about that?" Dede asked.

"It was all a lie!"

"How do you know?" I asked, ignoring my mother.

"Because a week later I happened to be at Sassoon. I casually asked the receptionist if George Davila still worked there. At first the receptionist didn't seem to remember him, so I thought he might have used some other name. I began to describe him, and it turned out that our senior stylist shampooed heads for a living!"

"You're kidding!" we all gasped.

"He was fired because he was pilfering the salon's hair supplies and selling them at a discount out of his apartment."

"It's a good thing they didn't report him to the police."

"Or the INS. He's a TNT!"

"That's it!" my mother exclaimed as she gathered her things and took my hand. "We're leaving right now!"

"No we're not!" I said as I pulled her back. I was beginning to have a good time.

"They checked his Social Security number," Chinggay continued, "and found out it was a fake. No wonder he was very effusive in telling me how he was already a *sicenta*."

"Sixty?" I asked, confused.

"As in *sixty cents*. That's code for citizen," Dede explained to me.

"But look at him now. Look how everyone comes up to him."

"He's giving out something," I said as I craned my neck for a better view.

"Must be his calling card. He gave me one, but only with his name and number. He never gives anyone his address."

"But I thought you were friends."

"We are. That's why I'd rather not spoil his drama. Let's check out the buffet. I'm starving."

The buffet was two rectangular tables joined together and covered with green crepe paper cut to resemble banana leaves. There were huge platters of grilled fish, prawns cooked in crab fat, stuffed chicken, pork barbecue, and *pancit* noodles as well as clay pots of ox tail stew and a three-foot ice sculpture of a young woman dressed in a Philippine costume. Along the buffet line, people stopped to admire her, their admiration turning into malicious snickers as soon as they walked away. When our turn came, we understood why. Up close, her face was strikingly similar to that of Dr. Palaypay, minus fifty or so of the pounds she carried on her frame.

Just then a young girl behind me broke into sobs, upset by the pair of roast pigs flanking either side of the ice sculpture, their open mouths stuffed with caramelized apples.

"Sshh," said her mother, rubbing her daughter's back, trying to calm her down. "They're just pigs, you know. Here, have some."

The child shook her head and bawled even louder. Two men dressed in ill-fitting chef's uniforms served slices of the roast pig's bright orange skin and carved out tender fillets of its juicy red meat. As the line slowly moved along, the child pointed to the pigs and sniffled, "They look so sad."

We smiled as we helped ourselves to a little of each dish. Others piled food onto their plates, as if each serving would satisfy their craving for home, each bite a piece of the motherland. We were near the end of the line when someone bumped me from behind and I felt a slick, oily line sliding down my leg.

"I'm so sorry," said a woman getting down on her knees to wipe the sauce off my stockings and shoes.

"It's all right," I said, "I can wipe it myself."

The woman stopped. She was staring at my mother. "Ludy Dacanay?" she said.

"Yes, but I don't remember—" my mother said as I helped the woman up and shook her hand.

"I'm Marinella Blardony. Honey Parungao is my aunt. My mother is her older sister. I think the last time I saw you was at *tita* Honey's birthday party at the Kiyake Grill on Makati Avenue."

"I remember now," my mother said, becoming visibly uncomfortable. "Paquita is your mother. How is she?"

"She's fine. I work as a nurse at St. Vincent's Hospital. What a small world! I just got a letter from *tita* Honey telling me to look out for you, and here you are. So, how long have you been living here?"

"Oh, more than two years now. What about you?"

"Almost a year. No wonder I haven't seen you. *Tita* Honey told me how upset she was because you didn't even say goodbye. So what do you do?"

"She works at a graphics design agency in midtown," I replied forcefully.

"Are you a citizen or a green card holder?"

"Citizen," I answered.

"How lucky! Where do you live?"

"In Queens," my mother interjected.

"You're joking! Where in Queens? I live in Astoria. We could be neighbors. Let's get together. Here, let me give you my number."

Just then the lights dimmed as the drum rolls began. It was our chance to escape. She was still scribbling on my napkin when I grabbed it and said, "We'll catch you later," and hurriedly backed away. I held on to my mother's elbow as I guided her back to our table, looking behind me now and then to make sure that the woman hadn't followed us. My mother's skin was cool to the touch. My hands were clammy.

We reached our table just as a giant silhouette waddled onto the stage and the lights shone on Queen Luzviminda, dressed in a traditional Philippine gown. She stood in front of the microphone and reached into her bosom, pulling out a pair of reading glasses and a small piece of paper. As the drum roll faded, she thanked all the participating pageant sponsors and individuals who had made the evening a success, even, "last but not least, God."

Her speech was followed by a five-minute standing ovation, which finally stopped when she introduced Adonis Kislap, the evening's emcee and guest entertainer.

"I thought he was dead," I whispered to Chinggay.

Fifteen years ago, Adonis was the top entertainer in Manila. I remembered how our maids used to go crazy over him, pestering my mother to let them watch his concerts at the Araneta Coliseum. Now, here he was in a Queens restaurant, his belly bursting out of his beaded cummerband, singing selections from his old repertoire. The audience, the women in particular, went absolutely mad when he sang "*Peel*ings," the Morris Albert song he popularized many years before. The screams and howls didn't stop, not even when he had moved to the stage's far right corner, trailed by a single spotlight directly above him, to sing "Pearly Shells." The audience finally calmed down only when a movie screen descended from the ceiling, flashing montage images of the current Miss Pearl of the Orient–U.S.A. and her court when they were all infants. As the last frame faded from view, the screen disappeared back into the ceiling, and the stage lights were turned on in full force.

There stood the young women, a tiara perched on every head. They looked like stars trapped in the wrong galaxy. As Adonis announced their names, they took one step forward, an awkward movement greeted by rounds of applause. I was startled by Chinggay's overly spirited clapping directed at Miss Baroque Pearl, one of the youngest participants, now tottering on satin high heels. Then I remembered that it was gratitude, not adulation that dictated Chinggay's enthusiasm.

One by one, Adonis escorted a pearl down the runway for the traditional presentation before the judges. As each tried to maintain her balance and her poise, he serenaded them with unabashed gusto.

"We just bumped into Marinella Blardony, Paquita's daughter," I whispered to Dede.

"Honey Parungao's niece? What's Marinella doing here?" Dede asked.

"Working as a nurse at St. Vincent's."

"Did she ask questions?"

"She wanted to know what Mom did, where we lived. Wants to get together sometime. She gave me her number."

"Where is it?"

I handed her the napkin, and she promptly folded it into a thin roll. With a smile, she put one end to the candle flame and watched it turn to ashes. Then she turned to Mom and said, "Now you can relax and enjoy yourself."

"Frankly, I'd feel a lot better if I knew any other TNTs in this crowd," my mother said.

"Nobody goes around with a TNT sign hanging down his neck," Chinggay snapped from the side of her mouth. "Why would you want to know anyway?"

"It would be nice to know how things were going for them.

If their secrets were better than mine." My mother laughed, but Chinggay did not join her.

"Just because a person talks in a weird accent or isn't blond and pale doesn't mean that they couldn't have been born in this country. When I first arrived, it didn't bother me that people always asked where I came from. And here I am, American passport and all, and people still think of me as a newcomer."

"How did you become an American citizen?"

"The old-fashioned way, naturally."

"What do you mean?"

"I paid for it."

"How?"

"Cash, of course. These people don't take VISA. I married a cousin of a friend of mine for a small sum."

"But what about Chuckie? How did you manage to get a divorce from him?" my mother asked.

Chinggay's eyes narrowed. She got up from her seat abruptly, rushed out into the lobby, and headed straight for the ladies' room. My mother and I caught up with her just as the door was about to knock me off my feet.

"Chinggay! Chinggay! Where are you? What have I said?"

I heard heels tapping inside one of the cubicles. I went toward it, bent down, and quietly pointed to Chinggay's shoes. My mother tiptoed over quietly and stood outside the door. I inspected the rest of the cubicles to make sure they were all empty and locked the bathroom door.

When she came out, there were tears in her eyes and her eyeliner and mascara were streaking down her cheeks. "I caught them, Ludy. The two of them were taking a shower in my bathroom. They were making fun of me: the clothes I wore, the colors of my lipstick, my family. He said that sex with me was like having sex with a dog, except that dogs were more fun; that he couldn't stand my bad breath. And then—and this I can never forgive him—he said my body was a miracle of nature."

I watched the two of them through their reflections in the mirror.

"Who was the woman in the shower?"

"What woman? Chuckie was screwing Momoy, our gardener. Sisa's son!"

"Chuckie? Gay?"

"Remember how everyone said how lucky I was to have caught him, me a famous model but from a low-class family. I thought marriage would change him. Then I kept hearing about his fondness for the stable boys at the Polo Club. Momoy was not the first. But I never confronted Chuckie. I respected his privacy. Besides, he was the only man I ever knew."

My mother gently pulled her away.

"He was a good provider, he was kind. He never hit me. I just didn't want his homosexuality slapped in my face. But to have that whole thing happen in my home! That was too much. I had to leave."

We walked out of the ladies' room just as Queen Luzviminda was about to knock on the door. She was surprised to see us, especially Chinggay's red eyes and flushed cheeks.

"Her candidate lost," I said abruptly and walked past the stunned woman.

Dede was waiting for us in the lobby, and together we walked down Broadway. My mother decided to keep Chinggay company and together, we all rode the train into Manhattan in silence. At the Public Library, we got off and walked toward Macy's. At times, I heard Chinggay sniff. But mostly we saw taxis speeding through puddles. We made a right turn on 34th Street, walked down to Macy's, and paused at the entrance to the PATH station.

"Will you be okay on the train? Do you want us to take you home?" my mother asked.

Chinggay said she'd be fine. "But you want to hear something funny? I still think of going back."

"Why would you want to do that?"

"Because the feeling never goes away."

"Feeling homesick, you mean?"

"No. Feeling like a TNT."

27

"Caloy, I'd like you to meet my mother."

We were at the Odeon restaurant in downtown Manhattan for brunch. He was standing next to my mother, grinning. When my mother offered him her hand, he leaned over her and kissed her warmly on the cheek. I could tell she liked him instantly.

"Finally, *tita,* we meet," he said as he took a seat opposite my mother and next to me. I felt the touch of his hand brushing against my arm.

"So tell me, Caloy, how long are you in for?" my mother asked.

"Unfortunately just until this afternoon. I have to be back on campus this evening."

"I wish you were staying longer. I would invite you over to our place for dinner. I make the best *sinigang* soup with salmon heads."

"Caloy doesn't eat fish, Ma," I said. "He's a vegetarian."

"Since when did fish have anything to do with being a veterinarian?"

Caloy choked on his coffee.

"Not *veterinarian. Vegetarian!* It means he doesn't eat animal flesh."

"Oh, vegetarian. I know what that is. But aren't you a Catholic, Caloy?"

He cleared his throat. "I am. I stopped eating meat a couple of years ago."

"So what do you eat? Salads, grass?"

"Well, there are beans, tofu, and wheat gluten. Next time I'm in the city, I'll cook for you."

"When will that be?"

"In two weekends. As a matter of fact, why don't you and Viola come to my sister's place in Princeton? It'll be my niece's birthday."

"We can't. We have plans," I said quickly.

"*We* have?" my mother asked.

"Didn't you say we were going to visit Dede's relatives in Nyack?" I said urgently.

"But you said you didn't want to go, remember? When I told her that you weren't coming, she decided to cancel the trip."

"Perfect." Caloy smiled triumphantly. "Two weekends from now, we'll all drive over to my sister's."

I felt like kicking him but I was intercepted. As the waitress leaned over to pour me a glass of orange juice, a busboy walked by with a trayful of dirty dishes balanced above his head and bumped into the table next to ours, accidentally nudging the waitress, who lost her balance and spilled her entire pitcher of freshly squeezed juice all over me.

Caloy grabbed a napkin to pat me dry. My mother tried to get up, but Caloy told her to sit down, saying, "I'll handle this, *tita.*" But before he could get up I rushed to the ladies' room. There were bits of pulp all over my Max Mara outfit, on my arms, my shoes, and even in my hair. I looked as if I had just walked through a blizzard of oranges.

I had known that something bizarre was going to happen—the brunch was such a weird idea to begin with. It wasn't even my idea, it was Caloy's. I knew that it spelled disaster, but we hadn't seen each other since I arrived.

I tried to keep him away. I cajoled, argued, dangled threats, but to no avail. Caloy was not easily dissuaded. I told him that my mom hated to give up her Chinatown shopping on weekends, that he'd have to chauffeur her home because on Sundays she refused to take the subway after 4:00 P.M., that she was picky about restaurants. Whenever the phone rang, I made sure to answer it before she did, just in case he was on the other end of the line.

He called while I was in the shower. Next thing I knew, my mother was all excited, accusing me of keeping Caloy away from her. She even tried to make a joke out of it: If he's a citizen, perhaps I should marry him, become a citizen. I told her to leave my personal life alone.

"Where were you when God was giving out a sense of humor?" she asked sarcastically.

"Inside your stomach, hiding!" I shot back.

Whenever I met a man for the first time, the first thing that occurred to me after I had run through the requisite checklist of age, birth sign, educational attainment, and physical appearance was how long it would take for any of them to annoy the hell out of me. After a couple of dates, five usually being the max, each man began to reek of something achingly familiar. I began to see my father in every man I dated. Their gentle flirtations became his come-ons, their smiles were straight from his duplicitous lips, their compliments were his lies, their faces his bloody head.

It had happened before, and now it was happening again. Except that, unlike any of the other men, Charles "Caloy" Magno Austria had one major advantage: distance. He was sustained by a perception filtered through the lens of my last memory of him in Manila, an image that underwent so many transfigurations that by the time I saw him again, he might as well have been Kevin Costner.

He wasn't going to go away easily. But what if he ended up like my father? What if he turned out to be a jerk like the rest of them?

"You know," I finally said to him, "you're the only guy I've known who's ever shown an interest in meeting my folks."

He laughed, a sweet, possessive laugh. "That's because none of them ever got that far."

"Wrong. It's because *I* didn't let them."

"That's what you like to think," he said.

We didn't speak for a few moments, but I heard him breathing on the other end of the line. Then, very gently, he asked, "Are you afraid that your mom won't like me—"

"She wouldn't dare!"

"—or like me too much for your own good?"

"I have to go now, Caloy. There's an incoming call. Take care, and I'll catch you later!"

Right up to the day of the brunch, my mother never mentioned Caloy's name again. I was dead sure she was playing games with my brain.

"Why were you so hostile back there?" my mother asked as we waited for Caloy to get his car out of the parking lot. "You should have seen your face. I thought you were going to kill the busboy. I think the last time I saw you lose your temper was—"

"Getting drenched by a pitcher of orange juice is not exactly my idea of fun."

"But even before that you were cranky. You were unladylike. Men get turned off by that."

"I am not turning him off!"

"Well, you weren't exactly Miss Charming."

As if on cue, Caloy appeared from around the corner in his two-door BMW. He got out of his side to open our doors, helping me into the backseat, then helping my mother into the seat next to him, strapping her seatbelt in place. The three of us rode into Queens in silence. When we got to the apartment, he asked my mother if he could take me out for a short drive. At that point, he could have asked her for anything. Including my hand.

Caloy and I drove back to Manhattan. The car windows were down, the sun roof was open, and the CD player was going full blast. As the wind blew through my hair, I felt it lift away my dour mood, and toss it into the slate-gray waters of the East River.

It was a nice Sunday afternoon, and I was beginning to regret that Caloy's visit was ending soon. Maybe we could take a stroll around Central Park, share an ice cream at Rumpelmeyer's. We were quiet as we made our way across the Queensborough Bridge. Over to our left, I saw the sun setting just behind the Statue of Liberty. This was the Manhattan I loved best, when the view was only from above and never from below, when it slowly went from brilliant orange to deep violet, and cars on the FDR Drive turned on their headlights, one after the other, like fireflies on parade.

As we got off the bridge and made our way toward Central Park, all I could think of was wrapping my arms around Caloy's neck.

"You didn't have to be so cozy with my mother." The words slipped out, hopping about like a hundred toads.

Caloy had been singing along with the music. He turned down the volume and said, "I happen to like your mother."

"Now she thinks we sleep together."

Caloy slammed on the brakes as a biker dashed across in front of us.

"How could she know what we do?"

"It doesn't matter what she *knows*. It's what she *thinks* that counts."

"She's been in New York for a while now, hasn't she? She can't be that narrow-minded!" He looked thoughtful. "Well, if it bothers you that much, I'll just talk to her."

"And tell her what? 'Really, *tita,* Viola and I have never slept together!' My mom is not stupid. You'll just make it seem more obvious that we've slept together."

"But we haven't!"

"That's beside the point, and please keep your voice down. Whatever you say will only make you look defensive, which is exactly what she expects."

"So we should just sleep together and not worry about what she thinks. Let her think whatever she wants."

"Anyhow, you didn't even talk to me. You completely ignored me."

"When?"

"Brunch, two hours ago."

"That's not true. I tried to draw you into the conversation, but you seemed to be more interested in sulking over your outfit. You didn't even laugh at my joke."

"The two of you were so gross."

"I thought that her *pan de sal* story was charming. Why didn't you ever mention it before?"

"Why don't you date my mother? You seem to have a lot in common."

Caloy chuckled as he tried to take my hand. But I was quicker, and he ended up grabbing the shift stick instead. We crossed Central Park and came to a stoplight. I felt Caloy turn to look at me and then straight ahead again. When the light was green, he said, "This has nothing to do with your mom." His voice was dark and ominous.

"I don't know what you mean."

"I'm not playing games, Viola. You can do that with everyone else, but not with me."

"How dare you," I said angrily, "how dare you use that tone of voice on me!"

"Admit it. You're afraid."

"Afraid?"

"You're afraid I'm going to end up just like your father."

"Don't drag my father into this. You know nothing about my father!"

"I know his reputation with women. I know about his mistress and his two boys. I know about the PCGG and Tee Pak Long."

"For someone who lives in Cambridge, you sure get around. Tell me, Tom Brokaw, what else do you know?"

"I also know about your mo—"

"What about my mom?"

"Come off it, Viola. I know she's a TNT. That's why you delayed this brunch for so long."

He pulled over to the curb and, turning his body sideways, raised his right knee onto the seat. "I'm surprised you didn't trust me enough to know that I would never have held it against your mom. Considering what your father has put her through, you should be pretty damned proud of her."

I grabbed my shoulder bag and placed my hand on the door handle. Then, very slowly, I turned to face him, remembering every detail. "Go away and don't ever bother calling me again."

I opened the door, slammed it in his face, and started to walk away, looking for the nearest subway. As I neared a corner, I heard Caloy's voice. "Hey, Viola."

I turned around to face him with a half-smile, my hands on my hips. "What?"

"Chicken!" Caloy shouted as he sped away, his tires screeching on the asphalt.

I didn't go back to Queens right away. I decided to go to Chinatown instead. My mother and I would have gone there if it hadn't been for—. I shook my body to get rid of the afternoon. It was good to be around a crowd, to bury myself beneath all that density. I wasn't in the mood to resurface. At least not for now.

I walked down Mulberry Street to Sam Fook Lee's grocery store, where my mother and I usually did our shopping. It was busy as usual, and I found myself among other Filipinos buying jars of shrimp paste, cans of Ligo sardines, bags of jasmine rice, packets of tamarind soup mix, and bottles of *patis*. The carts filled up quickly, the checkout line getting longer and longer.

The last time my mother and I were there I surprised her by displaying my expertise at haggling. I was so good that her regular fish vendor told her never to bring me along again if she ever wanted to buy fish from him. He was joking, of course.

After shopping, we always went to a noodle restaurant for a late lunch. I remembered our conversation from the last time we went. It was about her work, something we rarely talked about for obvious reasons. I didn't want her to think that what she did for a living was okay with me. Not that *that* would have stopped her. But now she and I had more or less reached an understanding about it—the less said the better. There were times, though, when she couldn't help herself and talked about her work.

Every morning, I let myself into the Steinbergs' apartment. I go directly to the refrigerator door, where she always leaves a note enumerating my specific tasks for the day. Her list always amuses me, not so much for the content, but because the notes actually exist. Who the hell does she think she's dealing with? I always tell her that I don't need the list. "But you might forget," she insists. I begin to deliberately forget a task or two, without being obvious. I simply say, "But it isn't on the list, Mrs. Steinberg."

The Steinbergs are quite easy to work for. She breezes in and out of the apartment and talks on the phone when she stays long enough. I never see her read, yet she's always bringing home a new book or some artsy coffee-table book. She has an opinion on just about everything, but she gets them from Regis and Kathie Lee. Her husband is a sweetheart. He's henpecked. He spends most of his time in his study, sitting in front of the computer. He wears a toupee. For an Upper East Side apartment, it's okay. But it's not my taste. My collection of Steubens and Lladros is better than hers. I rearrange the furniture and the decor whenever I become bored with the way they look. She questions me about that. I tell her that direct sunlight isn't good for her stuff. She leaves me alone until the next time. She needs to understand that I am not just a housekeeper. After all, I haven't been a Manila socialite for nothing.

I lingered in Chinatown long enough. It was time to go home. When I got to the apartment, she was sitting in front of the TV watching *Wheel of Fortune* and plowing through a pint of coffee ice cream.

"Your father called," she said.

"He's here?"

She shook her head. "He called from Manila."

"What did he want?"

"It's on the machine. He left a message."

My father's voice sounded terribly hoarse. If my mother hadn't told me it was he, I wouldn't have guessed. He said that he needed my mother as a character witness in his case with the BIR and the PCGG; the Galaxy board of directors was preparing to oust him. Unless she sent a signed affidavit or made a court appearance, the PCGG would take over the bookstore and auction off its assets. I thought of the mango tree, and some other child eating its fruit. I thought of our house, and another family making their life there.

I replayed my father's message over and over, unable to think straight. My mother just sat there, hypnotized by Vanna White. I wanted to shake her, turn her inside out, rouse her into something warm and alive instead of this passive mass occupying space. I looked down on the floor and saw a crumpled piece of paper lying around my feet. It was the picture of our house. I bent down to retrieve it. I smoothened out the creases and returned it to the place it came from.

28

Caloy was playing tough. No letter, no message on the machine, nothing. It had been a month since we last saw each other. Didn't he miss me? Shit, I didn't miss him one bit. How dare he not call! His silence was driving me out of my mind.

My mother didn't mention him at all. It was as if she had never met him. She didn't fool me. I *knew* she was dying to find out about him. About us. I imagined sending her telepathic waves that said, *Ask me about Caloy, ask me about Caloy.* To her credit, and my disappointment, she didn't. Our language was a litany of platitudes.

It wasn't as if we weren't on speaking terms; we just didn't have anything to say to each other. She didn't even seem worried about my father's call. The one other time my father came up in one of our conversations, she was more interested in setting the record straight about herself and her family history, many years after the fact.

"I was already pregnant when your father and I got married," she said one evening.

"I know."

"And you never said anything?"

"It wasn't my place."

"You could have at least given us some hint that you knew *something*. How did you find out?"

"I found my birth certificate after you left. I did a little arithmetic."

"Well, at least we got married."

"Would you still have gotten married if you weren't pregnant with me?"

Her face softened. "I truly loved Dado. Having you sealed that love for us." It had been a long time since she called my father by his name instead of the insults she usually reserved for him.

"I'm sure it advanced your timetable a little."

"When your father and I told your *lolo* I was pregnant, he was so livid with anger I thought he was going to die right then and there. 'How could you do this to your beloved mother's sacred memory?' he accused me. He said that I was humiliating the family, I was hurting him, and most of all, I was betraying my mother. At one point he went to my mother's portrait, knelt before it and asked for her forgiveness because he had raised an immoral daughter. As if she could have actually swooped down from the sky and yanked your father's manhood away from me. But I have no regrets whatsoever. I was only sorry that my father died before he ever had a chance to hold you in his arms."

"What did he die of exactly?"

"It was a simple heart attack. His first and last. He was so heartbroken."

"Not the cassava pie?"

"He was in the middle of eating his cassava pie when it happened."

"You know you can divorce Dad, don't you?"

"That would make it easy on him, wouldn't it? If he really wanted one, he could always ask for it."

"Does it upset you that I knew about your pregnancy all along?"

"Not upset."

"Upstaged, maybe?"

"You were so curious about where babies came from."

"Why are we talking about this now? Is there anything else I should know?"

"No, nothing more. Are you angry with your father for leaving us?"

Am I angry with you for leaving me?

"Not angry. I just know that I would never let something like that happen to me. You always told me that."

"Yes, but at the time I may have been speaking out of *my* own anger."

"And you're not angry anymore? After all that he's done? I find that hard to believe."

"There's no way of predicting what can happen in a relationship."

"Maybe *predict* is not the word. *Prevent* would be more like it. A relationship based on preventive measures."

"You make it sound like a prescription for bronchitis. The only way you can prevent anything is not to have any relationship at all. Is that what you want?"

I didn't answer. I deliberately turned away, afraid that my answer was there for her to see.

One day, when I was by myself in the apartment, I picked up the phone, punched in Caloy's number and wished that he wouldn't be there. Three and a half rings later, I heard the music of "Don't Worry, Be Happy." And then his recorded voice.

What should I say? "Hi! Viola here. Sorry!" then hang up?

That should do it, shouldn't it? Too abrupt? Tell him how I feel? On the machine? Better to do that in person. *Think quickly, Viola, the beep is coming.* This is insane. If he really cared as much as he said he did, I shouldn't have to be doing this. Damn! This was not the time to get tongue-tied.

"At the sound of the beep, please leave a brief message."

Here it comes.

Beep.

"Cock-a-doodle-doo!"

Click.

The next time Caloy was in New York, we decided to spend the day in the city, walking around the Upper East Side. It was a Friday afternoon, and the next day we were all going out to Princeton for his sister's party. I was nervous about meeting his family for the first time. I splurged on a new outfit to make a good impression. I set aside my worries and decided to let tomorrow take care of itself. Today, I was simply feeling good, lucky even. I could tell that something auspicious was about to happen.

Caloy and I were meandering along Third Avenue when I saw, across the street, a woman dressed in a white uniform, cleaning up after the dog she was walking. I was about to say something like, "And you thought we had uniformed maids only in Manila," when something about the way the woman held her shoulders and was vigorously cleaning up the mess reminded me of someone very familiar.

I held tighter to Caloy's arm and began walking firmly in a different direction.

"Hey, I thought we were going—Look, Viola, doesn't that—isn't that your mom?"

As if she heard us, my mother looked up, turned in our

direction without looking at us directly, and resumed her leisurely walk. Caloy's arm suddenly felt as stiff as a baseball bat.

"I thought she sold life insurance."

"Only in her spare time," I lied as I buried my face in his chest, crying. Stupid dog. I had completely forgotten about that stupid dog.

I said that I needed to go back to Queens. He understood, squeezed my hand, and offered to drive me back, but I said no. I needed to be alone. I called my mother and said I was going home ahead. She sounded disappointed. Then she asked if everything was all right. I answered yes. Everything was fine. After we hung up, I was short of breath. I needed air. Needed to be away from my mother.

When I returned to our apartment, I lay on my bed, soaking in the faded smell of my pillow's rose perfume. Everything in my mother's apartment smelled like that: faded, tired, frayed. I don't know if the smell had to do with the mothballs she used or was simply the process of a slow, decaying life. I had seen the nets advancing toward my mother, toward us, and yet somehow we had managed to elude them. Next time, we might not be so lucky. There might not even be a next time.

And then, because I was struck by the absurdity of what our lives had become, I began to laugh. Loud, uncontrolled laughter. I was still laughing when my mother walked into the apartment, confused, I could tell, by my mood swings. But that night when she and I had gone to bed, I felt a familiar pain tapping lightly on my chest. It was the pain of the inevitable.

Early the next day, I told Caloy that we weren't going to join him after all.

29

I am standing outside The Royal Court building on 84th Street and Third Avenue, the building where the Steinbergs live. They have an apartment on the twenty-second floor. After many excuses and delays, I am finally here to meet my mother (and the Steinbergs).

I straighten the pin on my lapel and fix my jacket collar. I carefully fluff the lace handkerchief in my breast pocket to make sure that it looks just right. It is the same one that my mother wore on her First Holy Communion. I don't know why, but it mattered to me to be well dressed. I quickly open my compact to check my lipstick and see that a line has gone astray just below the lower lip. I dab at it with the tip of a tissue. I pat my hair into place and see that a few strands of grey have already appeared. It is age tweaking my vanity. I look at my watch. It is four-thirty in the afternoon. My mother doesn't expect me until half past five.

A uniformed doorman comes out to greet me. He asks if I am there to see someone. I tell him I am going to 22-A, the Steinbergs' apartment. He leads me to the elevator, tipping his cap. I could live in a place like this.

At the twenty-second floor, the elevator opens to a small hallway. Only two doors lead to the two apartments on the floor. The door to apartment A is open. I decide to walk in. A life-size portrait of Elfrida Steinberg stands in the center of the foyer, and the first thing that impresses me is her hair. It is very red. It has taken over the painting. I can see what my mother means by the woman's lack of taste.

I walk through a narrow hallway, stopping by the first open door I see. It seems to be the study. There are floor-to-ceiling shelves filled with books. The walls are a combination of stencil and mahogany woodwork. The floor is covered in a lush carpet of apricot and mocha ribbon patterns wrapping themselves around floral sprays of ruby red and leafy green. Off to one side is a black lacquer secretary with a computer monitor blinking in the darkness. I see a man hunched over the keyboard, snoring. I assume it is Mr. Steinberg.

I decide to look at the rest of the apartment. I imagine my mother hard at work. I imagine having no imagination. Various artworks adorn the walls. From the living room, I can see across the East River to Long Island City where we live. Framed by the striped raw-silk curtains and gleaming from the angle of the sunlight, it actually looks picturesque.

I wonder what Elfrida would say about our house in the Philippines, about my mother's collection of Steubens that far exceeds hers. About my mother's beloved garden. I wonder if Elfrida even knows exactly where my mother came from. Then I hear voices. I decide to move closer to the source.

"Look," shrieks the louder voice. "Look what they've done to this jacket. It doesn't fit me anymore. I can never wear it again!"

The voice that responds is meek and contrite. It belongs to my mother.

"I even reminded them to cover the buttons, as they always do."

"Never mind the buttons. Do you know how much this cost me?"

"I'm not lying, Mrs. Steinberg," my mother tells her meekly. I take a step closer to the door. I can see Elfrida Steinberg standing next to the refrigerator, her copious chest undulating with her every intake of air. Her portrait does not do her justice—she is far uglier in person. "I don't understand how this could have happened. I've never had problems at Lucky's before."

"You took my Chanel to Lucky's!" Elfrida's voice shatters the sound barrier. "Are you retarded? I told you to take this one to the Imperial. I even reminded you to talk to James because he handles all my Chanels."

"That's not what you said. All you said was, 'This goes to the cleaners,' so I took it to your usual place."

"This is a Chanel, Lou," she says coldly, hurling the jacket on the floor. She is about to say something more, but she stops midway and sees me.

"And who are *you*?" she asks imperiously.

My mother twirls around, looking absolutely stupefied.

"Viola!"

"You know her?"

My mother is next to me, holding my hand. Her fingers are cold. "Mrs. Steinberg, this is Viola, my daughter." My mother addresses the woman as if she were Queen Elizabeth.

Elfrida proffers her hand to me, but I refuse to take it. She suddenly looks lost. She avoids my eyes and smiles a silly smile. When she speaks, her voice is all charm and sweetness.

"My goodness, Lou, the two of you could pass for sisters! How are you, dear?"

"Fine."

My mother merely stands there, looking back and forth between Elfrida and me.

"Well, I better run now," Elfrida continues. "Viola, dear, come and visit any time. You may go now, Lou. By the way, feel free to take home some of that leftover veal and *tiramisù*. We'll continue the rest of our conversation tomorrow."

"Thank you," my mother says.

My cheeks are tingling from the woman's acid tongue. As we walk out the door, Elfrida calls back to my mother. "Don't forget to hang that jacket by the coat closet."

My mother and I walk along 84th Street and head toward Fifth Avenue. We do not speak. We turn left on Fifth, barely avoiding a Rottweiler who growls and bares its teeth at us. I say to the dog in Tagalog that "*I will turn you into barbecue*" and smile at the owner who says, "Thank you." It is the beginning of the rush hour. Two patrol officers—a man and a woman—stand on the sidewalk, sipping from paper cups.

"They should help direct traffic," my mother says.

"How could you take her leftovers after the way she just talked to you?" I snap, pointing at the plastic bag.

"She was probably just having a bad day."

"There you go again. Making excuses. You didn't even stand up for yourself. I can't believe that you let her dump on you. You took it as if you deserved it! Is she always like that with you?"

Pedestrians file past us nonchalantly, barely noticing us. Before my mother can answer, I yank the bag from her arm, walk up to the trash can and toss it inside. "That's where it belongs."

My mother rushes to bend over the can, picking up the same bag "before some homeless person takes it." She hooks the plastic bag to the safety of her wrist.

"Never, never throw food away again, Viola," she scolds me. "If you have a problem with leftovers, no one's going to force you to eat them. And to think that I was going to tell you the good news. Just this morning, Mr. Steinberg offered to sponsor me."

"Sponsor you for what, Ma? A job on Wall Street? A membership at a country club in Connecticut perhaps? But that's not it, is it? They're sponsoring you as a domestic helper, aren't they? They're sponsoring you as a *maid*!"

My mother stalks away like a four-year-old, her coat billowing in the wind. I let her. It is a pleasant fall afternoon. The maple and gingko trees are putting on a dazzling display of orange, magenta, and copper. The air is crisp, and I can detect a faint smell of cinnamon. I see that she is three blocks ahead of me. Her pace has slowed to a stroll. She expects me to catch up with her. Ten years ago, she would have thought nothing of pulling my hair and slapping my face with her hand or the sole of her slippers. In public. Public humiliation was her only way. Her parents did the same. I don't remember how many times my face was pushed around, rubbed against a variety of textures, including sandpaper.

I don't chase after my mother. She can sulk all she wants. I know she knows I am right. The truth hurts. It always does.

30

My mother and I hardly talked throughout the subway ride. She couldn't even bear to look at me. When a rather obese woman took the empty seat next to mine, edging me closer to my mother, my mother's reaction was revulsion. At me. I mumbled an apology, but it was clear that my mother was not interested in what I had to say. Already she was immersed in her Sacred Heart novena prayers, nervously twisting a rosary between her thumb and index finger. I put on my headphones and decided to stand for the rest of the ride.

When we arrived, my mother immediately changed into her housedress and went to the bathroom. Standing before the medicine cabinet, she pulled back her hair with two hairpins and dipped her fingers into a jar of Pond's cold cream. With the three fingers of each hand pressed tightly against one another, she began to move them in small, brisk circles. Round and round they went, crossing her cheeks, her nose and her forehead, fingerpainting the creamy texture of the makeup remover and the eye shadow into a gray gloss all over her face. When she was done, she reached for a tissue and wiped it all off.

Seeing her without any makeup on, I wished I had never

met her at the Steinberg apartment. I had managed to postpone it for so long that she had stopped inviting me to come and visit. She had ceased to use that girlish, beguiling voice of hers whenever she wanted something, and I couldn't stay away. Something about the Steinberg apartment, a force much stronger than I, was pulling me closer and closer, getting harder and harder to resist.

I could not forget the sight of my mother receiving the full brunt of Mrs. Steinberg's wrath. There was a submissive expression on my mother's face. Her voice was subservient and frightened. It was the look of *our* maids when *she* used to scold them. Seeing her standing in front of Mrs. Steinberg, my blood began to curdle. As if *I* was a TNT, hiding and lying like my mother.

From the bathroom, my mother went to the kitchen to heat up our dinner of stewed ox tongue, paella, and the veal from Mrs. Steinberg. I tried to apologize for my earlier outburst, but she dismissed it with a perfunctory flick of the hand. "Occupational hazard," she said.

Our dinner was a carefully choreographed avoidance of the time bombs ticking within us. We sat there repeating to each other the exact same stories, laughing as if we were telling them for the first time. Except that we both knew that the laughter was a clever disguise for our stubborn refusal to acknowledge that life was indeed passing us by.

My mother was talking about the shows she had recently watched on TV, her excitement momentarily displacing the afternoon's fiasco. She became the European marquesa giving Elsa Klensch a grand tour of her villa in Positano, the Manhattan socialite kissing Luciano Pavarotti on the cheek, the Wall Street investment banker giving financial advice.

Television had become my mother's world, an accessible, portable object she could control. Tune in, tune out—my mother never had to exert herself. I had thought that the reason she rarely went out to the movies, a concert, or a museum was because they were too expensive. Or that her friends were always busy, or weren't interested in the same cultural things. That's what she always told me, and I believed her. Until she told me in the next breath how she had just splurged on a pair of turquoise pumps to match her turquoise silk scarf. "I really needed them," she said. "They were on sale," she added when I replied, "I thought you had no place to go."

Neither the lack of money nor the lack of friends had anything to do with her watching TV. In her confusion about the world she lived in, spinning from one make-believe world to another, she had lost track of what was real and what was not. Television was her reality. If she wasn't careful, it would swallow her, and she'd be gone forever.

It hit me right then that I didn't want to lose my mother.

"How's Caloy?"

Her question was so unexpected and direct that I found myself confiding in her. I was surprised by how I could admit to her the very things I found hard to admit to myself. She sat there without talking, responding with an occasional gentle nod, slight frown, or faint smile. When I was finished, I steeled myself for her reaction, regretting the impulse that had driven me to open up in the first place. *Had she understood me at all?* When she stood up and disappeared into the main room, I felt she had just slapped me with her indifference. Instead she came back with the phone and handed it forcefully to me: "Tell him what you have just told me!"

"Why?"

"Because you have to get rid of the ghosts."

"What ghosts?"

"Not all marriages end up like mine. Not all men are like your father."

After dinner, she announced that my father had called again, asking for her help in his case with the PCGG. Her voice was calm as she recounted his call, and there was no trace of malice. Then she stopped, and her shoulders stiffened. I became acutely aware of the expression on her face. She let go of the plate she was rinsing and bent her head, crying softly to herself, her head swinging in small movements from side to side.

"What's wrong, Ma?" I asked.

She turned away from me, crying harder. I pulled her gently away from the sink, and we walked over to her bed. I propped her up against a stack of pillows, lifted her legs, tucked her under the covers and ran back to the kitchen to get her a glass of water. When I returned, she was wiping her eyes with the corner of a pillow case. She accepted the drink without a word. I sat quietly next to her and gently massaged her shoulders. They were as stiff as death.

Suddenly, she pushed the covers away, sat up, and leaned over her legs and groaned. In a moment of panic I bent over her and pulled her straight up. Large teardrops rolled down her face and formed a wet map on the lap of her housedress.

"Let me get you a towel," I said.

I tried to get up, but my mother pulled me down. "No, I'll be fine. Just sit here beside me. Please."

I put my arm around her and held her tightly.

"I knew it, I knew it!" she said. "I warned your father from the very beginning about dealing with the Chinese. But of course he didn't listen to me. Now this has happened. We could lose everything that my father built, and the mango tree that came from my mother's." She buried her face in her hands and cried more. Finally, she leaned against the bed, placed an arm across the top of her head and stared up into the ceiling.

"Didn't you once tell me that your father was buddy-buddy

with a Senator Bimbo or someone who had connections with the PCGG?"

"When I left, Senator Bimbo was under investigation himself."

"You know, once I leave this country, I can never come back. I could never get another visa from the U.S. embassy. Especially not now."

"But what if you didn't have to come back?"

My mother sat up and looked straight at me. "You don't actually expect me to live in Manila again, do you? How do you expect me to survive?"

"You call *this* surviving?" I said, aware of the escalating tones in our voices.

"Why can't you accept me for who I am?"

"You don't even know *who* you are anymore!"

My mother got up and stood in front of me. "How dare you talk to me like that! Your life doesn't hold a candle to what I've been through. You don't even have the decency to be grateful."

"Grateful for what?"

"For saving you. I left Manila in order to save you!"

"You weren't saving me. You were saving yourself!"

My mother backed away and stood next to one of the windows. "I can never go back. Ever!"

"Why not? You still have the bookstore. We still have our house. *Yaya* Charing, Eladio are still there. It will be as if you never left. Isn't it time you stopped living like a fugitive?"

"It's not a crime to be an illegal alien."

"No, but passing yourself off as an American citizen is."

"What do you know? You're not a TNT!"

We looked at each other, and I saw myself reflected through her eyes. I didn't like what I saw. It was a premonition of what I could become. My mother stood up and began to pace back and forth. Then she stopped and shook a fist at the ceiling. "I'll be damned if I'm going to live in the same city as your father and his *whores*!"

She said *whores* over and over again. I was stunned by the anger that had finally found its natural voice, the voice that had been muffled for a long time. When my parents were still together, we were forced to live under a cloud of silence, feigning ignorance of the hurt and betrayal that casually floated around. Throughout my father's womanizing, my mother tried to conceal her anger. She was always protecting my father's reputation. She didn't want to admit that she had married the wrong man.

On the rare occasions that she did say or do anything—like the times she saw my father's girlfriends smiling confidently from the society page—she'd put black halos around them with a marker pen, as if that gesture was enough to throw them back to where they came from. That didn't stop my father's womanizing. By the time I was fourteen, she made sure that *I* knew their names, addresses, phone numbers. My mother didn't want these women to remain nameless or faceless. "Look at them and remember," she would say, destroying my father in my eyes. It was the only way she could fight back. Often, I thought she had succeeded.

I wished she had thrown that fish head at my father a long time ago. But she continued to serve him the disgusting thing. Now here she was screaming *whores* like a fishmonger, finally admitting to herself the ultimate injustice that my father had inflicted on her. It was neither the womanizing nor the bastards he had fathered. In leaving my mother, my father had thrust her into a life that she would never have *chosen* for herself.

"Let it go, Ma."

"WHORES! WHORES! WHORES!" she screamed.

"The past is the past!"

"The past will always be with me."

"You can't live with it forever."

"And what? Pretend that it doesn't hurt? That it never hurt? If it hadn't been for me, your father would have been nothing. It was my father who set up the business. It was my father who took him in to work for us. Your father was just a poor nobody. And this," she said, hurling the moldy Godiva candy at the walls, running to the kitchen and throwing the *tiramisù* on the floor, spinning round and round with her arms raised to the ceiling, "this is what I get!"

That night, I heard my mother toss and turn in her bed, go to the bathroom and to the kitchen for a drink. I was equally restless. Her apartment had suddenly become too small for both of us. It was better to wait for the sleep that never came.

My mother left early the next morning; she looked rather relieved that she was leaving. As she walked out the door she said, her eyes glazing over, "Don't worry about me. God will provide."

I was overcome by an intangible fear for my mother, not so much what others might do to her, but what she might do to herself. I was afraid that she would not be able to save herself in time. After breakfast, I called Caloy but he wasn't there. I tried several times, but the result was the same. I reached for the phone book and flicked through the back pages until I reached the blue section.

As my fingers traced each section, I read, "Easy Reference List, New York City Government Offices, State Government" and finally, "United States Government sections A, B . . . E, F . . ." until I reached the letter "I."

I found the number I was looking for and jotted it down.

From the corner of my eye, I saw an old postcard on the floor. It was a picture of the Statue of Liberty. I bent to pick it up, flipped the card over, and recognized a familiar handwriting.

"My dearest Viola, I went to see the Statue today. She doesn't look so pretty up close but she is so tall. Someday, I hope to take you there. Study well. Don't forget to pray. I love and miss you very much. Kisses, Mommy."

I reread the card several times and put it under the frame of a picture of my family. Then I went to the phone, lifted the handset and punched in a number. The line was busy. I tried again, anticipating another busy signal, but this time the line on the other end began to ring. My hand tightened around the phone.

"Hello. You've reached the INS. Ask Immigration System. For English, press ONE, now."

ONE.

"Because your call is important to us, our officers are available during normal business hours to assist you. However, since there are so many callers, please allow our recorded messages to first provide you with the information you might need. For information about your local INS office, U.S. passports and visas or how to obtain INS forms, press ONE. For instructions on how to speak with an officer, press TWO."

TWO.

"In order to be able to speak to an officer, you must first select and listen to at least one subject message. The option to speak directly with an officer is only given at the end of each subject message. We will now return you to our main Ask Immigration Directory. Press ONE."

ONE.

I listened to the drone of the cold, monotone voice as beads of sweat rolled down my neck. Why wasn't calling the INS the same as calling an airline? The waiting period was the same. I missed the voice selling exotic white beaches and cheap tickets.

No weather report. Thank God I didn't have to do this every day, pressing one number after the other, being passed from one electronic message to the next, feeling totally alienated from humanity. I was suddenly light-headed.

With the phone sandwiched between my neck and shoulder, I sifted through the pile of papers again, scattering them in the air like giant pieces of confetti. *Where was that darned postcard? Where was Caloy?* I scrambled down to the floor, shuffling through more folders and more postcards, spreading them around me. Where's Liberty? Liberty could not be found.

I was desperate. Then I remembered where she was. From the corner of my eye, I saw the frayed edges of Liberty's crown and grabbed the card. As I held on to it tightly, I heard, *"For information about how to report illegal aliens, press ONE, TWO."*

ONE, TWO.

31

I was on the phone for an hour. *Tik! Tik! Tik!* the line went, tap-dancing its way into my ears. Many times I wanted to hang up. *Life was not meant to be on hold forever!* But whenever I came close to putting down the phone, I'd hear an electronic beep and hang on.

What if I was a handcuff away from being kicked out of this country? *You can't touch me, asshole! Can't you see I'm on hold?*

"May I help you?" came a female voice.

"Thank God! I thought I'd be here forever," I laughed. "Hello, hello? Are you still there?"

"Yes, I'm still here," the voice said evenly. "Did you want to *ax* something?"

Ax? What *ax?* The lady's *ax* broke my concentration. I lost my nerve. I remembered seeing my mother bend over the trash can and lift the bag of leftovers.

"Um, well, I wanted to report an il-"

"Yes?"

"I'll just call back."

Click.

When I hung up, the phone refused to leave my hand, sticking to my fingers like part of my anatomy. Stop. *Give it a rest, Viola.* Then, taking a deep breath, I lifted my hand oh so gently and— It was free! My hand hung limply by my side, my pulses running at 100 mph.

Was I really about to report my own mother? *What was I thinking?*

The phone rang. Oh shit, it's the INS! They've traced the call back to me. Let it ring. They can talk all they want on the answering machine. Tomorrow I'm out of here! America is history. Shit! I sound just like a TNT. *Stop cursing, Viola!*

"Hi, it's me!"

Mom?

"Hello, hello, I'm here," I said frantically, fumbling with the buttons on the answering machine as my mother's recorded voice played in the background, "You have reached 555-0-4-4-5. Sorry you missed my call bu—" It was strange to hear two versions of my mother speaking at the same time, one reality overlapping with the other.

"Oh, you're there! I'm glad I caught you." She said, quickly adding, "Why are you home? I thought you said you were going out. Are you sick or something?"

"No, I'm fine. So what's up?"

My mother laughed, her voice playful and exuberant. *Had she been drinking?*

"You know, I just realized after all this time"—she laughed some more—"that I have never showed you where my parents were buried."

"What?"

"I know it sounds strange, but it just occurred to me that I've never taken you there. The cemetery in La Loma. You see, I stopped visiting my parents' graves shortly after you were born. I couldn't stand the traffic, and there were just so many other things to do. Can you imagine how lonely their graves must look? I just hope that the mango tree is still there. I remember exactly where their graves are. Right next to the Monteverde mausoleum. That's where my parents are buried. They had bought the lot as newlyweds even before they bought one for their house. My parents wanted to be buried together. It's funny that here they were, about to begin their lives, and instead they were preparing for their deaths. But they didn't have enough money to pay for two, so they only bought one. Their tombs are one on top of the other."

"Listen, Ma—"

"Two for the price of one," she said, her voice suddenly taking on a hypnotic, almost magical tone. "My parents planted the tree together, shortly after they were married. I can still clearly remember the day of her burial. I wasn't that much older than you. My father and I were sitting alone on the stone bench a few feet away from her grave. Everyone else had either left or gone back to their cars to give us some privacy. It had begun to drizzle, but my father refused to leave the cemetery. He couldn't leave her. He knew that once he did, it would really be over for him. So he and I just sat there saying nothing to each other. I'm sure that had I not been around, he would have just as easily jumped in with her. When I looked at my father, I saw tears running down his face. Like a waterfall. You know, my father wasn't the emotional type, or at least, he never showed his emotions to anyone. Certainly not to me. But there he was, crying like a little boy. I felt embarrassed. I took his hand and held it. I was afraid to say anything. Then you know what he did? He got up, pulled something out of his pocket, and went to the mango tree. I didn't follow him because I thought he was going to, you know, relieve himself. So I waited. He stayed by the tree for such a long time I thought he'd fallen asleep. He was so drunk, you know, all of us thought he'd never make it through the burial. I picked up his handkerchief, which he had dropped on the ground, and quietly walked up to him. You know what he was doing? He was carving a big heart on the trunk of the mango tree, and inside the heart, he had carved three initials: my mother's, his, and mine. Imagine that? My initials. Then he turned to me and said, 'Together always.' That's all he said. To my father, it was enough that he had carved a heart on the tree trunk. He didn't need to say anything more."

My mother paused. In the past, our telephone conversations were a safe hiding place for us, a sanctuary from which neither of us had to emerge in order to engage in hand-to-hand combat. We both knew that neither of us would survive a confrontation of great magnitude. But perhaps we had outgrown our fears. The time had come to face each other. I began to cry. So did my mother. I saw our tears rushing through the wires and flowing into the whirlpool of our common pain.

"You see, I was always afraid of my father," my mother was saying as she swallowed quick gulps of air. "I was so afraid of him I couldn't give him love. Not even when he died. But that part of my life is over now. I have to stop being afraid. I have to stop running away. It's time to lay *my* ghosts to rest. Because when my time comes—"

"Oh, Mom, please—"

"Because when my time comes," she said firmly, "I want to be buried with my parents. Not anywhere else. Certainly not among strangers. I don't want to be alone anymore."

"I understand."

"I mean it, Viola. Promise me that. Promise me!"

"Cross my heart—"

"—hope to die."

"Hah?"

"Viola, why do you keep saying *hah*? Is that all you've learned since you came to New York?"

"I don't understand."

"I just quit my job. I wish you had been there to see the look on Elfrida's face. After I left home this morning, I felt a soreness in my stomach. It was as if someone had been jumping all over my body. I thought I'd never make it to work, but I did, barely catching the N train into the city. When I walked into the Steinbergs' kitchen, the coffeemaker was percolating and Elfrida was sitting on a stool, going over the Metropolitan section of the *Times*. Next to her were two empty coffee mugs waiting to be filled. In all the time I worked for them, Elfrida never offered me breakfast, much less a cup of coffee. I found her sudden generosity eerie. At that very moment, she reminded me of a tub of lard boiling over. I apologized for being late—she gets very upset if I'm late by even five minutes—but she wouldn't hear any of it. 'It's not the end of the world, Lou,' she said as she poured us some coffee. She began to tell me how much she enjoyed meeting you. How you were so smart and pretty. Then she apologized for her outburst. Of course I said it was all right. I told her that, speaking from experience, you don't scare easily. She liked that line and laughed. But her laughter was cheap and low. And then she said something about making it up to me. At first I didn't understand what she meant, so she said it again. 'Since I can't use the jacket anymore, and I hate to part with a Chanel, I'm willing to sell it to you at a fraction of the price I paid for it. After all, you are a part of my household.' I told her that I would have no use for it. I'd rather die than own anything that belongs to her. But you know what the bitch said? She said, 'Oh, not for you, silly. For Viola. I think she'd look absolutely smashing in it.' Then she placed the jacket carefully on the table. Seeing it there, something just snapped inside of me.

"The next thing I knew, I put my cup down and slowly removed the jacket's plastic wrap. Elfrida sat there, looking entirely pleased with herself. I walked to one of the drawers where the knives were kept, pulled it open, and removed a cleaver. Before Elfrida could stop me, I began to slash the jacket, ripping its lining apart, putting holes in every part of its sleeve. Elfrida clambered down off her stool, her eyes looking like extra-large black olives, breathing heavily with every pound her body was forced to carry. I thought she was going to go into cardiac arrest. I cut the jacket into more pieces, hem for hem, cuff for cuff, button for button. There was no sound in the kitchen other than the sound of fabric being rent. I was unstoppable. *Jab! Jab! Jab!* my fingers went. I swear, Viola, I was having the time of my life. When it was over, I said, 'I guess Viola can't wear this now.'

"I returned the cleaver and gathered up my things. She was hysterical, and she kept shouting for her husband to come. But the man's deaf. She threatened to call the police, but I simply ignored her. Then she screamed, 'I'll report you to the INS! I know where you live. I have friends in high places. You and your daughter will be out of this country in twenty-four hours!' The woman was desperate. But I wasn't afraid of her. I said, 'You touch my daughter and I'll put your head through a garlic press!' And for my finale I added, 'I'll call your friends and tell them *all* about your liposuction.' And I left."

"Just like that?"

"Just like that."

"What's going to happen now?"

My mother laughed again, her sense of humor finally breaking free. She had laughed more in the past fifteen minutes than I'd ever known her to.

"I've decided to go home."

"Hah?"

"There you go again. I said I've decided to go home. I'm going back and I'm firing your father!" She laughed wickedly.

"When did you decide this?"

"Oh, around two years ago." She laughed again.

"Are you sure?"

"There's nothing for me here."

Then my mother hung up. She was gone. The line was empty. I called Caloy again, and this time left a message on his machine. "My mother and I are going home," I said. "I'll be waiting for you in Manila." I was still holding the Statue of Liberty postcard. I thought I had dropped it. As I stared at Liberty's face, I could hear the plane revving its engines and gathering speed, and my mother's voice humming "Good Morning, Starshine." I saw the plane lift itself off the ground and tilt backward, its huge body heading for the sky. Somewhere inside was my mother. She was finally going home. To me.

Epilogue

MY MOTHER IS TELLING ME ANOTHER STORY. *She begins by saying, "It is that time. I am in the delivery room of the Manila Doctor's Hospital. I scream to the nurses that I don't want the anesthesia. 'Don't put me to sleep,' I beg them. The nurses ignore me. Just another hysterical mother-to-be, their eyes say. One woman lifts my hospital gown and proceeds to shave off the hair from my private parts. Another holds me down by my arms and feet because I am kicking around too much. The nurses whisper to me in their lullaby voices. It will be easy. You won't feel a thing. It will be over in a snap. My head screams, 'You're all worse than Satan!' I am not afraid of the pain. I want to feel my child passing through me. The pain is my redemption. Then my head aches because the scream is trapped inside. It is struggling to set itself free, but my head is harder than that. Nobody listens. The needle slips into my skin, so faintly it is almost imperceptible. Immediately, I find myself adrift among waves; it is a dark and starless sky. When I wake up, I see a tiny plastic crib being wheeled in. 'Here she is,' says a nurse. At that moment, everyone vanishes from the room except for you, lying now in my arms, wrapped in layers and layers of white cotton voile. You are fast asleep. Your hands are covered in white cotton mitts. I feel your softness through the blankets, your unblemished skin glowing like a beacon of purity, your smell untouched by the outside world. I start to cry. I remember the curse of my own birth. Through my tears I see the full moon outside my window. It is rising over the horizon. I am suddenly filled with a sense of power. I will protect you from the curse. That is all you ever need to remember."*

Of all my mother's stories, this is the story I love most of all.

—Manila